The Promise

MATERIALS FOR CHRISTIAN EDUCATION

PREPARED AT THE DIRECTION OF GENERAL CONVENTION

The Promise

BY PAUL THOMAS

ILLUSTRATED BY HOWARD SIMON

THE SEABURY PRESS

NEW YORK

Contents

The Promise

CHAPTER ONE

Moving Day

"Magurk, get off the sofa so the moving men can carry it out. Come on now—OFF!"

Whenever Mr. Parker spoke, Magurk obeyed. So he leaped off the sofa—right in front of two men carrying out the piano. He jumped out of their way and knocked over two lamps that were standing on the floor. This made him so nervous that he put his head down and ran for the peace and quiet of the back porch.

But he never got there.

Magurk hadn't taken more than two leaps and a bound when he crashed into the baby of the family, Sammy, knocking him flat on his back. Sammy didn't know whether to laugh or cry, and ended up doing both. Magurk didn't know whether to run or sit, and he ended up doing neither. He lay down to think it over.

Boy-oh-boy, he seemed to be saying to himself, *it's just one of those days!*

"Magurk, what are we going to do with you?" Mrs. Parker picked him up and carried him to a corner out of everyone's way. "Now you lie there, and not a whimper out of you until we're all moved."

That's the way it had been all morning. "Magurk, get off of this." "Magurk, get off of that." "Magurk, get out of the way." He tried to stay out of the way, but it seemed as though there were a million people in the house all going in different directions. Actually, there were only nine people in the house (five Parkers and four moving men), but when you're always in the wrong place at the wrong time, nine can seem like a million.

Magurk checked his new resting place. Nothing behind him but two bare walls. No furniture to be moved.

It seemed safe enough, so he put his head between his paws and watched the fun.

Magurk was a flop-eared beagle who had come into the Parker family as a puppy many years ago. In fact, he arrived on the same day that Mrs. Parker brought Jack and Suzanne, the twins, home from the hospital. Magurk didn't know how he happened to have such a strange name. There must have been times when he wished he had a name like Pal or Rover, but when he first knew that people were calling him by name, they were calling him "Magurk." So, "Magurk" it was, and that was the name he answered to.

Magurk may not have thought his name was very special, but he certainly thought his family was. The Parkers were the best family in the whole world, and he was ready to fight any dog who said they weren't. The Parkers thought Magurk was the best dog in the world —most of the time, that is. There were times when they weren't too sure of this, and these were the times Magurk wasn't sure whether he was a Parker or not. For example, take the day that he chewed up Mr. Parker's leather gloves, and Mr. Parker threatened to get rid of him.

Magurk closed his eyes. He could still see Mr. Parker starting the whole thing by shaking those gloves in his face. *What a time that was!* he thought.

This is the way it happened: Every night when Mr. Parker came home from work he would first kiss everybody and then he would shake his gloves in Magurk's face, and Magurk would jump and bark and snap at them. Everyone would laugh and have a good time— especially Magurk. One evening while the family was eating supper, Magurk saw the gloves lying on the floor and, stalking them like a true hunting dog, pounced on them. He shook them with his teeth. He threw them over his head. He held them in his paws while he rolled over on his back.

And then in came Mr. Parker!

The next day, the twins cornered Mrs. Parker at the lunch table.

"Mother, it just isn't fair," said Suzanne.

"It sure isn't," Jack agreed.

Magurk knew what was coming. You see, he slept in the twins' bedroom and, on the night of the glove-chewing, they had kept him awake with their serious talking. All Magurk had wanted to do was go to sleep and forget about the whole thing, but the twins wouldn't let him. It was very late by the time they agreed to speak to their mother in Magurk's defense the next day.

"How was Magurk supposed to know that the gloves

weren't to play with?" Suzanne walked up and down like a lawyer she had seen on television.

"Yeah," said Jack. "He didn't know what they were because dogs don't wear gloves. Nobody ever told him they weren't a toy like a ball or a stick."

"Mother, Magurk won't chew gloves any more because now he knows he's not supposed to—don't you, Magurk? Give him another chance, pleeeeze." Suzanne made "please" sound as long as three words.

"And besides," said Jack, "if he goes, we go." He sat back and folded his arms, looking very stern.

"Oh dear! We certainly wouldn't want that." Mrs. Parker thought for a minute. "I don't think it *is* fair and, you know, I suspect that Daddy doesn't think it's fair either. Daddy was probably really mad at himself for dropping the gloves where Magurk could get them."

Jack and Suzanne had sat down opposite their mother, listening very closely. Magurk cocked his head at the three of them. Mrs. Parker continued talking.

"We all do that sometimes, don't we—act mad at somebody else when we're really mad at ourselves? Why Jack, I remember the day you broke the wing of your model airplane and then got mad at little Sammy when he wanted to play hide-and-seek with you. And Suzanne, do you remember the time you were ironing your doll clothes and burned the wedding dress? Oh my, but you were angry with me when . . ."

Suzanne interrupted her mother. "Gee Mom, don't make a federal case out of it. I remember."

Mrs. Parker smiled.

"Just because your father and I are grown up doesn't mean that the same thing doesn't sometimes happen to us," she said. "I think Daddy knows that he wasn't fair last night, and I'll bet that there'll be no more talk about getting rid of Magurk. You run along now and play, and don't worry about it."

Mrs. Parker was right. When Mr. Parker came home that night (after he had kissed everybody) he started to shake a new pair of leather gloves in Magurk's face.

"Oh no we don't," he said with a laugh, and quickly stuffed them back in his topcoat. He then pulled a red rubber bone out of the other pocket and bounced it across the living-room floor for Magurk to chase.

"Bones are for dogs," he said, "and gloves are for daddies. If dogs sometimes get a little mixed up on this, daddies certainly shouldn't. Isn't that right, family?"

Everybody laughed.

* * *

Sometimes a little complicated and hard to understand, thought Magurk, watching the refrigerator being carried out the front door, *but a wonderful family—the best in the world*.

His thoughts were interrupted by a hard yank on his tail, and he turned his head just in time to see Sammy start to throw the full weight of his forty-three pounds down on top of him.

"C'mon, Magurk, let's fight. Everybody's too busy to play with me. You're all that's left." Sammy gave Magurk a real wallop with his hand and followed this by butting his head against Magurk's ribs.

Any other time, Magurk would have been up and going—racing around the dining-room table, barking at Sammy, chewing at his shoes, rolling with him on the floor. But not today. Magurk knew when he was well off. He had been in enough trouble already. So he just lay there and let Sammy do all the work. After about five minutes of being pushed and pulled, Magurk wasn't at all surprised when Sammy put his thumb in his mouth and fell fast asleep beside him.

"John, come and look at this. Isn't that the cutest thing you've ever seen?" Mr. and Mrs. Parker stood over them and smiled. Jack and Suzanne came and stood next to them.

"That's when he's nicest—when he's asleep," said Jack.

"Oh Jack, you don't mean that about your brother."

Mrs. Parker rubbed her hand on Jack's head. "Anyway, we're all packed and ready to go. Daddy, you carry Sammy. Come on, Magurk—into the car."

Outside, it was a sunny August day. The moving van had just left. A crowd of neighborhood friends stood around the car to say good-by.

"I promise I'll write you every day," Suzanne said to one little girl.

Jack was giving advice. "You better give up on the Reds, boy. Without pitching, they're dead. Dead!"

Mr. Parker started the car and backed it out of the

driveway. Everybody was talking at once. "Good-by." "Come back and see us." "Don't forget to write." "We'll miss you." As they drove slowly down the street, nobody in the car said anything. Suddenly, Jack wound down the window and stuck his head out.

"So long, you meatheads," he shouted.

Magurk noticed that there was one little tear rolling down Jack's cheek.

CHAPTER TWO

The New Home

"Oh Mother, it's so wonderful to have a room of my own."

Suzanne jumped up and threw her arms around Mrs. Parker's neck. "Now I won't have to live with *him,*" she added, sticking out her tongue at Jack.

"Ha!" Jack snorted. "Think it's going to make me mad not having to live with a girl? I couldn't have stood living in the same room with you for one more day . . . not

11

for one more minute . . . not even for one more second. And even that would be too long."

"I'm surprised that you two have managed to live this long," laughed Mrs. Parker. "The way you talk, one would think that fifteen minutes together would kill you both."

"Mother!" Suzanne stamped her foot on the floor. "It's not a laughing matter. You don't know what it's like to live with a boy . . ."

"I've managed to live with your father for some time now," interrupted Mrs. Parker.

"Daddy's not a boy, he's a man—and that's different. But boys! Mother, you just don't know. You just don't know! They're so messy. They don't want anything to look pretty—always leaving their things lying around. And the stuff they want to keep in a bedroom—oooh!"

Suzanne moaned and buried her face in her hands. Then she looked up quickly. "Do you remember the time Jack wanted to keep frogs in our bedroom?"

"They weren't frogs," corrected Jack. "They were toads."

"Toads? That's even worse. Oh Mother, it was . . . it was . . ." Suzanne hunted for the right word and then blurted it out, "It was horrible!"

"Oh yeah? Well, let me tell you something, *sister,*" Jack replied, spitting out the last word as though it tasted bad. "I'd rather live with toads than with girls. If I'd had to live with you much longer, I'd have to begin wearing skirts. I wasn't sure sometimes whether I was a boy or not —all those fairy curtains and ruffles on the beds and bottles of horrible smelling perfume on the dresser. Ugh!"

"Boing, boing." Mr. Parker, who had entered the room in the middle of this conversation, hit the bottom of a pan with a spoon. "O.K., you two," he said, "there's the bell ending Round One. If you're so overjoyed to have your own rooms, why aren't you both upstairs straightening them up? Come on, let's get moving."

"Bet I get my room finished before you do," shouted Suzanne.

"Bet you don't," cried Jack.

Laughing and pushing each other, they raced for the stairs. Magurk ran after them barking furiously.

"Not so much noise," Mrs. Parker called after them. "Sammy's still asleep."

Mr. and Mrs. Parker stood and looked at the living room. It was a mess. The whole house was a mess. Although the moving men had brought the right furniture to each room, none of it had been put in the right place.

And nothing had been unpacked. Mrs. Parker sighed. Mr. Parker smiled at his wife and gave her a kiss on the cheek. She smiled and patted his hand.

"Let's go, gal," he said. "There's enough work here to keep us busy for a week."

Without saying anything else, they began pushing furniture.

Upstairs, not much work was being done. The twins were busily daydreaming. Mrs. Parker had let both Jack and Suzanne plan how to decorate their own rooms. "John," she had said to Mr. Parker, "I think when you get to be their age, you're old enough to decide what kind of a room you want to live in." Mr. Parker was not quite sure, but finally gave in when the twins promised that they would live with their decisions—with no complaining. Although they made this promise confidently, both Jack and Suzanne were secretly a little worried how their selections would *really* look.

But now, sitting in their own rooms, they knew! Each was certain that the right choices had been made.

Suzanne lay on her unmade bed and admired how well the white-painted woodwork went with the soft yellow of her walls. *Yes,* she thought to herself, *the white café curtains will be just fine, and the dark brown rugs beautiful.* She rolled over on her stomach and smiled as she imagined how pretty the bed would look with a white dust ruffle and the new yellow bedspread. ("A dust ruffle!" Jack had snorted when she talked about it with her mother. "Just like a girl. Just like a girl!")

"Well, I *am* a girl," Suzanne said aloud, "and girls like pretty things—not toads. Ugh!" With a shudder, she got up and began to unpack her dolls.

In his room, Jack sat on a cardboard carton and looked around. Magurk had jumped up on the bed and was curled up on a pillow. Jack had decided on a wallpaper with pictures of different sports on it. He hadn't been sure about the curtains, but had finally chosen dark blue ones with white sailor's rope and anchors and life preservers running around the edges. The curtains weren't up yet, but the wallpaper sure looked good to him. He gave the room one more admiring glance, and then stood up.

"What a room," Jack said with pride. "Why it's a real *man's* room." Magurk half opened one sleepy eye and then continued to drowse. It had been a hard day for him. "Well, you can sleep if you want to," Jack said, rubbing Magurk's head, "but I've got work to do. I guess I'd better start putting things away."

Jack began to put things on the shelves of his tall standing bookcase. On the top shelf went his models—two

jets, a battleship, and a Tom Thumb locomotive. Then
he came to his rock collection, and stopped to study his
favorite pieces—the rose quartz, the petrified wood his
uncle had given him, and the lava that came from Italy.
The coffee can with the holes punched in the top went
in the bottom drawer of his desk.

"Ha!" he said to Magurk who paid no attention to
him, "only a girl wouldn't know the difference between
a frog and a toad. Let's go out tomorrow and catch a frog
to put in the can. Or maybe a couple of crickets—'cause
they sound so friendly."

The baseball glove was his next discovery. Before he
packed it, he had rubbed it with special oil, put a ball in
the "pocket," and tied the glove around it. Now, he un-
tied the string and slipped his left hand into the glove.
"What a neat pocket," he kept muttering to himself as
he walked around the room slapping the ball into the
glove. Jack stopped by the window that looked out onto
the vacant lot next door.

A gang of about fifteen boys Jack's age were playing
baseball. Jack put both hands on the window sill and
watched. One boy had just swung at a pitch and missed.
("A sucker pitch," Jack muttered.) The next batter hit
a ground ball that went right through the second base-

man's legs. ("What a jerk," Jack sneered. "I could have fielded that with my eyes closed.") Jack watched for a few more minutes, making comments to Magurk all the time. Then he turned to Magurk, who was wide awake now, and started throwing the ball into his glove even harder than before.

"Aw, what do I care?" he said, wiping his nose with the back of his hand. "I wouldn't want to play with a bunch of bums like that anyway. We don't care—do we Magurk?"

Magurk was sitting up now, watching very closely.

"Listen Magurk," Jack said quickly. "I want you to get the picture. It's the bottom of the ninth inning of the final game of the World Series. The Yanks are ahead by one run and the Bums have the bases loaded with two out. Duke Snider is at bat and Ford is pitching. I'm Mickey Parker and—even though my bad knee is hurting something terrible—I'm playing center field. Whitey pitches (Jack wound up and threw), the Duke connects (Jack swung an imaginary bat), and it's a tremendous drive! It looks like it's going, going—but wait!!"

Jack ran backwards across the room toward Magurk. Just before he reached the bed, he threw his ball in the air and leaped up for a one-handed catch. Falling back-

wards on the bed, he cried, "A great, great catch by
Mickey Parker. We did it, Magurk, we did it. We saved
the game!"

"Children! Jack and Suzanne! Dinner's ready." It
was Mrs. Parker calling from the kitchen.

Jack and Magurk jumped up and started out the door.
Jack stopped and went back for one more look out the
window. The game was over. The vacant lot was empty.
Jack threw his glove on the bed.

"Aw, I didn't care anyhow," he said, and went downstairs.

Mr. Parker had built a fire in the outdoor fireplace and,
because none of the dishes were unpacked yet, they all
roasted hot dogs on the ends of long sticks that had been
cut from a willow tree in their back yard. Usually a picnic was a very happy time for the Parkers, but tonight
nobody said very much.

"It looks to me as though we're a very tired family tonight," said Mrs. Parker.

"Mother," asked Suzanne, "do we know anybody
here?"

"Well . . ." Mrs. Parker hesitated. "Well, not yet. But
then, that's what's so much fun moving to a new town—
meeting new people, making new friends. Why, in no
time at all you'll know as many people here as you did

at home—I mean, at our old house. Don't you think it will be fun?"

"I suppose so," said Suzanne, who didn't sound as though she supposed so at all.

Jack and Suzanne went to bed early. Magurk, who didn't know which twin's room to sleep in, curled up on the floor of the bathroom between the two rooms. Jack was just about to go to sleep when he heard Mrs. Parker talking to Mr. Parker downstairs.

"John, you know how happy I am you got the new job, and I think our new house is lovely, but already I miss the old house and all our good friends there. Why, we don't know a soul here!"

"Hey, girl, what's this?" Mr. Parker chuckled a little. "Remember what you told the kids. It'll be fun . . ."

Jack got up out of bed and tip-toed into Suzanne's room.

"Hey, Suze," he whispered, "are you awake?"

"Yes, come on in," she whispered back, sniffing just a little. "You heard what Mother said too, didn't you?"

Jack nodded as he sat on the edge of Suzanne's bed. Magurk jumped up and lay between them. After a long silence, Jack said, "Suze, did you ever feel that when you don't know anybody, maybe you're not alive?"

"Oh Jack, I've been so lonely all day. I mean, I like

my new room—especially not having to live with you—but I miss all my friends. I feel as though I'm in a television set—moving and talking, but not being real."

The twins both leaned over and hugged Magurk.

My goodness, he thought, *sometimes I'm glad I'm a dog. I can make friends with another dog just by sniffing him. When you're a human being, you can't make friends until you know a person. Yes sir, being a dog has its advantages.*

CHAPTER THREE

The Baseball Game

"Hey, what are you doing?"

Jack looked up from where he was kneeling. A boy about Jack's age was leaning across the back fence. He was wearing a baseball cap which had twisted on his head so that it was shading his right ear and not his eyes. Behind him stood the baseball players Jack had watched from his window a few days before. All of them had gloves and some were carrying bats.

"Looking for crickets," Jack said and returned to his search, trying very hard not to pay any attention to the boys.

"What a dope," laughed one boy. "You won't find anything there except worms—and they don't taste as good as crickets." Everybody laughed.

"Well, then," Jack said quickly, "I'm looking for frogs."

At this, everybody laughed even harder. Two boys in the back laughed so hard they fell down and rolled on the ground. Jack's face got red, and he turned his back to the boys so they wouldn't see.

"Aw shut up, you morons," said the first boy. "Hey, what's your name? Mine's Roger."

"Jack."

"Jack, how about playing some baseball with us? We need another man 'cause Billy Parks had to go visit his grandfather."

"Oh, I don't know," said Jack with his back still to them. "I sort of wanted to find some crickets this morning."

"Maybe he doesn't know how to play," said the same boy who made the remarks about the worms. But this time nobody laughed. Jack jumped to his feet and strode over to the fence.

"Listen," he said, and sounded very angry, "my baby brother Sammy could play baseball better than you. The other day I saw you miss ground balls that a girl would have got. And hit! Boy, you could use a tennis racquet. Maybe I can't play very well, and then maybe I can. But I sure can play better than you."

"O.K., O.K.," said the boy. "You don't have to blow your stack. I was just wondering . . ."

"What are we going to do—waste all morning talking?" asked Roger. "Come on, Jack, get your glove. We'll wait for you."

"Well," Jack said thoughtfully, "all right—if you need me."

He walked toward the back door, acting as though he didn't care whether he played or not. Once inside the house, he sped past his mother on the stairs and shouted, "I'm going to play baseball." Back down the stairs he ran even faster, skidding to a stop at the door. He opened it carefully and walked out of the house just as slowly as he had come in.

"Come on, Jack," a couple of boys shouted. "We haven't got all day."

Mrs. Parker smiled as she watched Jack climb over the

fence and walk with the other boys toward the baseball diamond next door.

"Sometimes," she said to herself, "I wonder whether I understand my children. For two days I tried to get Jack to go out and play with the boys, and he absolutely refused. Today, I didn't say a word about it, and off he goes. I don't know. I give up."

Out on the baseball field, they were choosing up sides for the game. Roger and a boy named Pete had been named captains. Roger tossed a bat to Pete, who grabbed it with his right hand. Roger's hand went on top of his, and Pete's on top of Roger's, until Pete's hand was snug against the knob at the end of the bat.

"I win," said Pete. "I'll choose . . ."

"Wait a minute," interrupted Roger. "You haven't won yet." He took the knob of the bat by the tips of his fingers and swung it around his head three times.

"I win," Roger said, "and I choose Jack."

A big smile burst over Jack's face. Proudly he stepped up next to Roger. Quickly everyone was chosen except the boy who had made fun of Jack, whose name was Willy. It was Roger's turn.

"O.K., Willy, I guess we'll have to take you," Roger said glumly. "C'mon team, let's decide on positions. Jack, what do you play?"

"Second base," Jack replied.

"Jack is at second and . . ." Roger started to say.

"Hey, wait a minute," interrupted Willy. "I always play second."

"I said Jack plays second and bats clean-up," continued Roger firmly. "Willy, you're in right field and . . ." Soon everyone was assigned a position and the game began. Roger's team was first up.

When Jack came to bat, there was a man on second with two out. *Now I'll show them,* he thought. Pete was pitching. He threw two balls and then one right down the middle. Jack gritted his teeth and swung fiercely. He lifted an easy pop fly that the catcher hauled in for the third out.

"My foot slipped," Jack said to Roger who went out to his position without saying anything.

"Ha!" laughed Willy as he ran out to right field.

It was not one of Jack's better days. At bat, he managed to get one single with nobody on base and then was left stranded. Three other times he struck out and once hit an easy ground ball back to the pitcher. In the field, things were not much different: three errors out of six chances. And Willy had something to say each time Jack muffed a chance. When the game finally ended, Jack

breathed a sigh of relief and started walking for home, his head drooping just a little.

"Hey, Jack, wait for me." It was Roger. He caught up with Jack and walked to the fence with him. "Don't pay any attention to Willy—he's always like that."

"He made me kind of nervous," Jack said glumly. "I would have played better if he'd have just let me alone."

"Do you collect things?" Roger asked, changing the subject.

"Rocks."

"Rocks? What kind of rocks?"

"Oh, all kinds," Jack said, and then added, "I'll show them to you, if you'd like to see them."

"Let's go," Roger said.

Jack took Roger in through the back door. They met Mrs. Parker as she was coming down from upstairs.

"Hey, Mom," Jack said, "we're going upstairs to look at my rocks. Oh, I forgot—this is my friend Roger."

"How do you do, Roger," Mrs. Parker said. "You boys look pretty warm—and I'll bet you're thirsty. How about some juice and cookies?"

"Swell," Jack and Roger answered in unison. Realizing they had both said the same word at the same time, they began to laugh.

Roger stayed for lunch and it wasn't until almost suppertime that he went home. Not only did he see Jack's rock collection, but he played with Jack's models and looked at the pictures Jack had taken at camp last summer. They both ended up in the back yard on their hands and knees looking for crickets. They caught two in a pile of wood.

Supper that night was a happy time. Everybody seemed to want to talk at once. Jack was just about to bite into his second piece of chocolate cake when he turned to Mr. Parker and said, "You know, Dad, this is a nice town to live in. I think we're going to like it here."

CHAPTER FOUR

Sunday Morning

It was 6:30 in the morning. The front door of the Parker house opened cautiously. Jack popped his head out and looked up and down the street. Then came Suzanne's. Then came Sammy's. Together they looked to the right, to the left, and then the three pair of eyes rested on the thick Sunday newspaper lying at the foot of the front steps.

"Nobody will see us," whispered Suzanne. "Go get the paper, Jack."

"Yeah," echoed Sammy, "get the paper, Jack."

"I got it last week," Jack said. "It's your turn, Suze."

"I can't go out in these shorty pajamas, Jack," pleaded Suzanne. "What if someone saw me?"

"Yeah," repeated Sammy, "what if someone saw her?"

"Aw, who'd even care?" Jack was disgusted. "O.K., I'll get it this time—but then you have to get it the next two times."

Jack ran nimbly down the steps in his bare feet. Just as he got to the bottom, the front door closed quickly but quietly. Jack grabbed the paper and climbed back up the steps looking very determined. Kneeling down, he whispered loudly into the mail slot.

"Very funny. Ve-ree funny! All right, wise guys— open this door or I'll tear the funnies into a million little pieces. See! Here's the first piece."

Jack tore off a corner of the funnies and pushed it through the slot. The door opened quickly and he entered with an air of victory.

"I want the funnies. I want the funnies. I want the funnies." Sammy jumped up and down, shouting as loud as he could. Jack pounded him on the top of his head with the rolled-up paper.

"Sammy, shut up," Jack said sternly.

"You'll wake up Mother and Daddy," Suzanne added.

Sammy stopped shouting but kept jumping. Then he stopped jumping and took a swing at Jack that missed, sending Sammy sprawling on the floor. Both Jack and Suzanne pointed their fingers at him and began laughing. At first Sammy looked angry, but then he laughed with them.

"Here," said Jack, opening up the paper. "Suze, you and Sammy can have the funnies, and I'll take the sports page."

Sunday morning was a very special morning in the Parker household. Of course, the newspaper was always special, and Sunday was the only morning on which the children were allowed to eat in their pajamas.

Just as Jack was taking his last bite of toast, Mr. Parker said,

"You children better get a move on if you don't want to be late. Come on, I'll lead the way. Is the Parker Army ready?—A-tenn-shun!"

Everybody stood at "attention" while Mr. Parker made a sound on the table like a drum. Then, as he barked the proper military commands, the Parker family followed him out of the kitchen and up the stairs. Sammy and

Magurk brought up the rear, and Mrs. Parker stayed behind to put the kitchen in order.

Although Mr. Parker was the first person up the stairs, he was the last to come down. Even Mrs. Parker—who was the last to start getting dressed—finished before he did. Jack had called up to him twice and was about to call a third time when they heard him start down the stairs.

"Well, dig him!" Jack let out a long whistle.

"Oh Daddy, do you look sharp!" Suzanne said with admiration.

"Where are you going, Dad—to a party?" asked Jack.

It wasn't that Mr. Parker looked so different from any other time he wore a coat and tie; it was just that the family didn't expect him to be so dressed up on Sunday morning. Usually he wore his old clothes and, after dropping Mrs. Parker and the children at church, came back to read the paper or work in the basement.

"Why, I want to know," said Mr. Parker, acting very surprised, "is everybody so amazed just because a man puts on a coat and tie to go to church?"

"You mean," Jack said, sounding *really* surprised, "that you're going to church even when you don't *have* to?"

"Jack, don't be so smart! Daddy, I think it's wonderful that you're going to church with us." Suzanne threw her arms around her father's neck and gave him a big kiss on the cheek.

"Your mother tells me that this church has a family service—and I guess that we're not a family if I stay home. Magurk, I imagine that leaves you out—although maybe after they get us fathers to church, they'll start working on you dogs. Well, gang—let's go."

Magurk walked to the door with them and then went back to curl up on the couch. *What's so surprising about a dog being in church?* thought Magurk. *Hmph! I went to church once,* he said to himself, *even though I didn't stay very long. Ha! It took three men to catch me—but I was there!* With that pleasant thought, he went to sleep.

The Parkers sat together at the family service. Mr. Parker wanted to sit in the last pew. The children wanted to sit in the front pew. They compromised and sat where Mrs. Parker had wanted to sit all the time—right in the middle. Sammy, who sat on the end, kept sticking his head into the aisle, and Mrs. Parker was kept busy pulling him back.

Jack leaned his head back and looked at the ceiling. *This wouldn't make as good a ship as the other church,* he said to himself, remembering why the main part of a church is called the nave.

It was a pretty church, but very different from the one

they used to go to before they moved—although that was very pretty, too. This one was newer and more plain. Everything was straight and neat, and the whole church appeared to be moving up toward the sky. It *was* different, yet somehow it seemed very familiar.

Jack thumbed through the small red Prayer Book he had taken from the rack in front of him. Then he looked at the altar and the baptismal font. *Funny,* he thought. *It's different, yet it's the same.* While they were singing the opening hymn, Jack leaned over and whispered to Suzanne.

"Suze, do you kind of have the feeling that you've been here before?"

"Yes," Suzanne whispered back, a little bit embarrassed by Jack's talking when she didn't think he should. "Now shhh! and sing."

"How can I 'shhh' and sing at the same time?" Jack said and began to giggle. Suzanne turned her back to him and started singing even louder than before.

When the younger children left for their church school classes, Mrs. Parker went with Sammy, since this was his first Sunday in the new church. Later, the older children went to their classes.

"Do you want me to go with you?" Mrs. Parker asked the twins.

"Mother! Don't you dare! I'd be positively embar-rassed." Suzanne sounded disgusted.

"Sammy's the baby—not us," Jack added, and they stepped into the center aisle following the other children out of the church.

Some one smacked Jack playfully on the arm. Jack turned around quickly and was glad to see that it was Roger. As he turned, he also saw Willy, who stuck out his tongue at them. Jack grabbed Roger by the arm and pulled him ahead, leaving Willy behind.

On the way home in the car, all that Jack and Suzanne could talk about was Willy. In class, he had made fun of everything that anybody said, and once the teacher got so mad that he threatened to send Willy home. And, what was worse, Willy always seemed to aim everything at Jack and Suzanne.

"Had you done anything to make him mad at you?" Mr. Parker asked Jack.

"I talked back to him that first day we played baseball," Jack replied, "but he had it coming to him. Roger says so, too. Roger says that he's always like that."

"And even if he is mad at Jack," Suzanne added, "that's no reason why he should be mad at me. I didn't do anything to him."

"Well, I don't know," sighed Mr. Parker. "I guess it

would be a pretty dull world if everybody liked us."

After supper that night, Mr. and Mrs. Parker were reading the newspaper in the living room while the children watched television in the den. Suzanne got up off the floor and came into the living room. Taking the newspaper out of Mr. Parker's hands, she climbed up into his lap.

"Daddy, I liked us all going to church together."

"I'll tell you a secret, Sugar," said Mr. Parker, "I thought it was pretty nice too. Say, what did you talk about in your class—besides Willy?"

"Oh, about God's family being everybody in the whole world. While they were all talking about it, I got to wondering . . ." Suzanne paused for a minute. "You remember this morning when you said that our family wasn't complete unless you were with us?"

Mr. Parker nodded.

"Well," Suzanne continued, "I got to wondering whether God's family would be complete until everybody in the whole world went to church."

"I suspect that it won't be, Suze," Mr. Parker said, and gave her a big hug.

CHAPTER FIVE

In the Beginning

September was upon the Parkers almost before they knew what was happening.

The huge maple tree in their front yard began to turn from green to deep red before the twins realized that the warm weather was just about at an end. Suzanne didn't notice the seasons were changing until brown print curtains replaced the white cafés that had made her bedroom seem so cool during the hot months. The thought of leaves to rake was what made Jack aware that vacations, swimming, and baseball were over for the year.

The twins were sorry to see the warm weather end, but they thought each season was wonderful. Their favorite time of year always seemed to be the one they happened to be in at the moment.

For Suzanne, September meant school, piano lessons again, and Saturday afternoon outings with the Brownies. To Jack, it meant football games, burning leaves, and toasting marshmallows in the living-room fireplace. For these, he was quite willing for summer to end.

For the whole Parker family, this first September in their new home was the month in which they began family Bible reading.

It all started at lunch after their third Sunday in church together. Mr. and Mrs. Parker were discussing the sermon when Jack broke into the conversation.

"I got that all right," he said, adding quickly, "I think. But that Bible reading went by me like a supersonic jet. Wow! I heard it, but I didn't see it."

"I'm glad I'm not the only one, Jack," Suzanne said. "I thought everyone else understood it but me. It's nice to have company."

"Aw, a lot of kids don't understand it. When Mr. Hall talks about the Bible in his sermons, I understand it—

most of the time," Jack said. "But, when it just comes shooting right at you in church, all those words get me confused."

"Daddy," Suzanne asked, "do you have to be grown up to understand the Bible?"

"More grown up than I am," Mr. Parker replied, "because I'm with Jack. When the Bible's explained to me in a sermon, I understand it most of the time. But aside from that, it's usually Greek to me."

"I understand everything, and I want to go outside and play." Sammy, who understood a great deal more than most people thought—but not *everything*—slid halfway off his chair waiting to be excused.

"If you've finished your lunch, you may be excused, Sammy," Mrs. Parker said, smiling as he mumbled an "Excuse me" and dashed for the back door.

"I must admit that I'm in the same boat with the rest of you," she continued. "But, I wonder if we shouldn't *try* to understand it?"

"I try by listening real hard," Suzanne said, "but it seems that the harder I try, the less I understand."

"So do I," Jack agreed. "How else is there to try?"

"Well, if you all wanted to, we *could* read the Bible together—as a family, I mean." Mrs. Parker said this hesitantly.

"What!" Mr. Parker practically jumped out of his chair. "Mary, if I can't understand the Bible when a minister reads it to me, I certainly won't understand it when I read it to myself."

"At least we would be able to discuss the parts we don't understand," Mrs. Parker said. "Of course, we might need some help."

"If *everybody's* confused," Suzanne said, "who could help us?"

"I should think that Mr. Hall would be more than willing to give us some help," Mrs. Parker replied.

"Boy, I don't want to be the one who tells a minister that I don't understand the Bible," Jack said firmly.

"I'm with Jack," his father agreed.

"John, you know how you feel at the office when you explain something and everybody says 'Yes, yes' but they don't understand it at all," Mrs. Parker said. She then turned to Jack. "And Jack, you remember how angry you were when your cousin Jim said he understood how your model trains worked—and then ruined your transformer because he really didn't understand what you told him?"

Both Jack and his father nodded sheepishly.

"Nobody likes people to pretend they understand, when they really don't—especially about important things," Mrs. Parker continued. "I'll bet Mr. Hall would be pleased if we asked him to help us understand the Bible better."

"I think he'd be pleased, too, Mother," Suzanne said. "After all, ministers are people too, aren't they?"

Mrs. Parker asked Mr. Hall to come over for lunch on Saturday. Sammy, who was at a friend's birthday party, was the only Parker missing. For twenty minutes, everyone made polite conversation. Mrs. Parker kept nodding at her husband, as if to say, "Go ahead. Go ahead and talk with him about it." Finally, Mr. Parker took a deep breath and began.

"Rector, we have a very embarrassing request to make of you. As a family, we are forced to admit that we don't understand the Bible, and we need some help."

Mr. Hall sat back in his chair and laughed. The Parkers were most surprised. They expected him to be shocked and very serious.

"Praise God, you're an honest man, John," the minister said, and then quickly corrected himself. "No, you're an honest family. Why, if I had a dollar for every person in our town who pretended to understand the Bible, but didn't—why I'd have enough money to build our new parish house all by myself."

He leaned forward on the table and added, "I'll be

glad to help you, and there's no reason why you should be embarrassed. I wish more people would ask for this kind of help. Now, what did you have in mind?"

"Well, we had talked about family Bible reading . . ."

"Which would help us to understand the Bible better when it's read in church," Suzanne said, interrupting her mother.

"It certainly would, Suzanne," Mr. Hall agreed. "But, to read the Bible *and* understand it takes the right tools and a little bit of work. For example, which translation of the Bible do you have?"

"I don't know," Mr. Parker said, looking a little confused. "I always thought a Bible was a Bible."

Mrs. Parker went upstairs to get their Bible. When she handed it to Mr. Hall, he looked at the title page and said,

"This is the King James translation, which is the one we're all most familiar with. Its language is very beautiful to read and listen to, but its English is four hundred years old and often difficult to understand.

"The translation we sometimes use in church is probably best for family Bible reading," he continued. "It's the Revised Standard Version of the Bible. It was translated within the last few years and uses language that is up-to-date and more easily understood than the King

James. I have some extra copies over at the church, and I'll be glad to let you have one."

"Thank you very much," Mr. Parker said. "But, what's all this about work?"

"Although the Bible is written to whoever is reading it," Mr. Hall began, "it was written by (and written about) people who lived a long time ago. These people spoke several languages and had customs and beliefs that seem strange to us because they're different. If we are going to understand the Bible today, we have to know something about all of these things."

"Wow!" Mr. Parker let out a long whistle. "I don't have time for work like that. I'm a businessman. I have to earn a living for this family. Maybe we ought to read a simpler book than the Bible."

"Most of the work's already been done for you," the minister said. "In our parish library we have books that can help you in all these things. If you will give it just a little time each week, the Bible will soon become clear. What do you say, John? Will you give it a try?"

Mr. Parker sat back and thought for a moment.

"O.K., I'm willing. How about you, family?"

Everyone nodded in obvious agreement.

"Just one word of advice before you begin," Mr. Hall said. "Don't read the Bible as though it's a book of laws, or an arithmetic table to be memorized. The Bible is sort of a package of letters, letters written in love. I'll admit that sometimes these letters get a little twisted in delivery, but that doesn't change the general rule: read the Bible as you would read a letter from someone you love."

"You mean that we shouldn't say that we'll read three chapters each night?" Mrs. Parker asked.

"Oh, I won't say that you're wrong," Mr. Hall replied, "but it's better to read a bit and then talk about it. Ask each other, 'What's the man who wrote this saying?' and then, 'What is God saying to us through this man?' Far better that you should read one verse and understand it, than that you should plow through three chapters and not understand a word."

"Gee," Jack said, "I didn't think you could talk about the Bible except in sermons or church school classes. I thought we were just supposed to listen."

"Talking's a very important part of family Bible reading, Jack," the minister continued. "And one more thing. Don't think you have to read every single verse. In family Bible reading, it's often best to do a little skipping . . ."

"Do you mean that we can skip the parts we don't like?" Suzanne said.

"Oh, no siree, young lady," Mr. Hall said, winking at Suzanne. "Those are very often the parts we *should* read. I mean that you'll occasionally find two different versions of the same story—as in the stories of the Creation or the giving of the Ten Commandments to Moses. Both versions are very important to the professors who study the Bible in seminaries and colleges, but a family only needs to read one of them. The books I'll lend you will help you decide which one. Or, take the 'begat' sections," Mr. Hall went on.

"The *what* sections?" Jack asked.

"I'm sure you've heard them, Jack. 'So-and-so begat so-and-so, and he begat so-and-so, and he begat so-and-so.' They're the family histories of Bible people. Again, they're most important for Biblical scholars, but families can skip them without missing anything.

"And, then, you'll find that you won't want to read some of the stories in full. Instead, you will be able to tell them in your own words, reading just important parts from the Bible. I'll give you books that will help you all in this.

"My goodness, I've got to get back to the church for an appointment," Mr. Hall said, looking at his watch. "I didn't realize I'd been talking this long."

"Daddy," Suzanne said, "why don't you go with Mr. Hall now to get those books?"

"That's a good idea, Suzanne," Mr. Hall agreed. "Why don't you, John?"

"O.K.," Mr. Parker agreed, "let's go, Rector."

When Mr. Parker returned, he was carrying three
books, one of them a Bible. He sat down in his favorite
chair and began to read. Every once in a while, he would
say to no one in particular, "Why, I never knew that," or
"Isn't that amazing?" And once he read three whole
pages aloud to his wife. Mrs. Parker had to interrupt him
for dinner, but he was back at it as soon as dinner was
finished. It was the same thing Sunday afternoon and,

on Monday, he even took one of the books to work with him to read on the bus.

Jack and Suzanne were amazed at the time their father was spending on this.

Monday night at supper, Mr. Parker announced that family Bible reading would begin as soon as the dishes were finished. Jack and Suzanne applauded, and Sammy joined in, although he wasn't too sure what he was clapping for.

"Where'll we start, Dad?" Jack asked.

"Since this will be *family* Bible reading," Mr. Parker said, "let's start at the place where the family of God begins."

"Where's that?" Suzanne asked.

"Right at the beginning, Suze, right at the beginning."

*   *   *

Mr. Parker had just finished reading the story of the Creation of everything, when Jack wanted to know why man was made last and not first.

"Of course," Jack said, "the world had to be made first so that man would have something to stand on. But there must be more to it than that."

"There is more to it than that," Mr. Parker said, "but I'm going to throw the ball right back at you. If you were going to build a home, how would you go about it?"

"W-e-l-l," Jack replied thoughtfully, "I guess I'd make it a wooden house and I'd paint it white . . ."

". . . with green shutters," Suzanne added.

". . . and with green grass in the front," Sammy said. Since no one paid any attention to him, he said it again.

Ignoring Sammy's contribution, Jack and Suzanne went on to describe the house they'd build. They talked excitedly for a few minutes, then Jack said,

"I guess that's the kind of house I'd build."

"Me too," Suzanne said.

"Me too," Sammy agreed, "but only if there's green grass in the front."

"I think I'd like to live in a house like that—and I *do*," laughed Mrs. Parker. "So do you. You've described our house perfectly."

"Well, I wouldn't like to live there," Mr. Parker said, "because you've all left out something very important. Do you know what it is?"

They all thought very hard.

"Magurk?" asked Suzanne.

"That's close," Mr. Parker said, "but not close enough. You didn't put any people in your house. You forgot *us!*"

"Gee, that's right," Jack said. "It wouldn't be a *home* without people, would it? It would be just like that model house we looked at before we bought this. Remember that?"

"That house gave me the creeps," Suzanne shuddered. "It was so empty and lonely. It was all fixed up for living, but there was no one living in it. It was kind of . . . well, I guess kind of dead."

"We forgot peoples," laughed Sammy.

"We sure did," Mr. Parker said. "Does that answer your question, Jack?"

"I guess so," Jack replied hesitantly. "You mean that God made man because the world looked lonely without him? I guess that makes sense—the world *would* be lonely without people."

"It sounds as though God made everything the way we made our imaginary house, Jack," Mrs. Parker said. It seemed complete—but there was no one to live in the world. So God made man."

"That certainly is part of it, Mary," Mr. Parker added, "but don't forget that people are not made for houses. Houses are made for people . . ."

"Hey, wait a minute!" Jack interrupted. "You mean that God made the world *for* man, don't you?"

Mr. Parker nodded.

"That makes the Creation something special, doesn't it?" Suzanne said. "Sort of like a *gift*."

"That's about it, Suzanne," her father replied. "A gift. The Creation is a gift—from God to us."

CHAPTER SIX

Man Gets a Name

The Parkers were all set for their second night of family Bible reading. Mr. Parker sat in his favorite easy chair, with the Bible opened on his lap. Mrs. Parker and the two boys were on the sofa, and Suzanne—her arms wrapped around her legs—sat on the floor. Mr. Parker began to read.

And the LORD God planted a garden in Eden, in the east; and there he put the man whom he had formed. And out of the ground the LORD God made to grow every tree that is pleasant to the sight and good for food, the tree of life also in the midst of the garden, and the tree of the knowledge of good and evil.

A river flowed out of Eden to water the garden. . . .

"Oh, it must have been lovely," Suzanne sighed. "Just think—all the most beautiful trees and flowers of the whole world in one place."

"And how fragrant it would have been," added Mrs. Parker.

"Dad," Jack asked, "where is the Garden of Eden? Could we go there sometime?"

"Wow! That's a tough one," Mr. Parker said. "The Bible talks about its being near the Tigris and Euphrates rivers—and I could show those to you on a map. But I don't think there was a Garden of Eden, except in the minds of those who wrote about it.

"The stories of the Book of Genesis were first told around the campfires of the early Hebrew tribes a few thousand years ago," he went on. "Fathers told them to their children, and the children passed them on to their children. They were finally written down for the same reason they had been told: not because they tell us about geography, but because they tell us about God."

"Jack and Suzanne," Mrs. Parker said quietly, "these

stories came from people who had looked around them and seen all the beauty and goodness there is in the world, and they brought it all together in one place called 'Eden.' What they're saying to us is, 'Don't look for the Garden of Eden, because there isn't any such place. But look for the beauty and loveliness of Eden, because it's around you every day—and let this tell you of the goodness of God who made it.' Do you know what I mean?"

"Sort of like plays on television," Suzanne said. "They're not real, but they can tell us things that *are* real."

"I know what you mean," Jack said, "but I still wish we could visit it."

"So do I," laughed Mr. Parker, "but let's get on with the story."

And the LORD God commanded the man, saying, "You may freely eat of every tree of the garden; but of the tree of the knowledge of good and evil you shall not eat. . . ."

"That sounds like a pretty easy club to belong to," Jack said, laughing. "Anything you want to do is O.K., just so long as you lay off the knowledge tree. Boy, what a snap!"

"Oh, is it now?" said Mrs. Parker. "I know a boy who seems to insist on doing whatever anyone tells him not to do. Yesterday, this boy (and I won't mention his name) came home with his hands covered with paint from a fence that had a big sign on it that said, 'WET PAINT—DON'T TOUCH.' "

Jack laughed again, this time a little sheepishly.

"Some of the paint's still on my hands," he said. "I guess that if that man was anything like me, it would be pretty hard not to eat the fruit God warned him about."

"That poor man," Suzanne said sadly. "He's all by himself in the garden. He needs company. When does Eve come in?"

"We're getting to that," Mr. Parker said. "Listen."

Then the LORD God said, "It is not good that the man should be alone; I will make him a helper fit for him." . . . So the LORD God caused a deep sleep to fall upon the man, and while he slept took one of his ribs and closed up its place with flesh; and the rib which the LORD God had taken from the man he made into a woman and brought her to the man. Then the man said,

"This at last is bone of my bones
and flesh of my flesh;

she shall be called Woman,

because she was taken out of Man."

Therefore a man leaves his father and his mother and cleaves to his wife, and they become one flesh. And the man and his wife were both naked, and were not ashamed.

"You mean that girls were made out of one of our ribs?" Jack asked his father. "How'd they figure that?"

"Oh Jack, ribs don't have anything to do with where girls come from, do they Daddy?" Suzanne said, looking rather disgusted. "It's the same kind of thing we said before. These stories are not trying to tell us about geography, or even science. So don't ask silly questions. BUT, I was wondering . . ."

Suzanne thought very hard for a minute.

"Didn't they say something like that when cousin Betty was married?" she asked.

"About ribs?" laughed Jack. "Now who's asking silly questions?"

"Oh, don't be fresh! I mean the part about cl . . . clea . . . you know the word I mean."

" 'Cleave' is the word you're thinking of," Mrs. Parker explained, "and it *is* used at a wedding—when Holy Communion is a part of the service. Used in this way it means to . . . well, 'to keep together.' It's a 'belonging' kind of word, and since weddings are when two people ask God's blessing on their coming together to begin a new family . . ."

". . . then this part of the Bible should be used," Suzanne finished for her, "because this is the beginning of the whole family—well gee, of the whole family of man."

"Is that all settled for you, Suze?" her father asked.

Suzanne nodded her head. Mr. Parker then began to read about the serpent tempting the woman to eat the fruit of the tree of the knowledge of good and evil. "The more the serpent talked, the more she wanted to eat that fruit, so . . ."

. . . when the woman saw that the tree was good for food, and that it was a delight to the eyes, and that the tree was to be desired to make one wise, she took of its fruit and ate; and she also gave some to her husband, and he ate.

"Oh, oh," whispered Jack, "I have a feeling that was a mistake."

Then the eyes of both were opened, and they knew that they were naked; and they sewed fig leaves together and made themselves aprons.

And they heard the sound of the LORD God walking in the garden in the cool of the day, and the man and his wife hid themselves from the presence of the LORD God among the trees of the garden. But the LORD God called to the man, and said to him, "Where are you?" And he said, "I heard the sound of thee in the garden,

and I was afraid, because I was naked; and I hid myself." He said, "Who told you that you were naked?
Have you eaten of the tree of which I commanded you
not to eat?" The man said, "The woman whom thou
gavest to be with me, she gave me fruit of the tree, and
I ate." Then the Lord God said to the woman, "What
is this that you have done?" The woman said, "The
serpent beguiled me, and I ate."

"Who does that sound like?" laughed Mr. Parker.

"Who?" Jack and Suzanne said together.

" 'Jack, did you leave the back door open?' 'Not me,
Mom. It must have been Suzanne,' " Mrs. Parker said,
smiling as she imitated the children's voices. " 'Suzanne,
did you leave the back door open?' 'Not me, Mom. It
must have been Sammy.' 'Sammy, did you . . .' 'It must
have been Magurk, Mom.' "

"Boy-oh-boy," laughed Mr. Parker, "isn't that the
truth! The Bible's not so out of date as a lot of people
think. It's talking about people we know—in fact, it's
talking about five people and a dog that we know very
well!"

"Yeah," Jack muttered, "us!"

"Meanwhile, back in the garden . . ." Mr. Parker
smiled. "Let's find out what happens next."

"Whatever it is," Suzanne said, "I don't think the man and the woman are going to like it. I'd hate to have God mad at me."

"Well, God deals with the serpent first . . ."

"Because you have done this,
  cursed are you above all cattle,
  and above all wild animals;
upon your belly you shall go,
  and dust you shall eat
  all the days of your life."

"I guess they thought that in the Garden of Eden the snake had legs to walk on," Mr. Parker said. "This story seems to be trying to explain why the snake is the only land animal that crawls instead of walking on legs.

"God speaks to the woman next . . ."

"I will greatly multiply our pain in
  childbearing;
in pain you shall bring forth children . . ."

"Here the story must be trying to tell why mothers feel pain when children are born," Mrs. Parker suggested.

"Now," Mr. Parker said, "God turns to the man . . ."

And to Adam he said . . .
"Cursed is the ground because of you;
in toil you shall eat of it all
the days of your life;
thorns and thistles it shall bring
forth to you. . . .
In the sweat of your face
you shall eat bread. . . ."

"Boy, Dad, I always thought *you* were tough," Jack said with a whistle, "but this seems like an awful lot of punishment for eating a piece of fruit."

"Don't be too hard on God, Son," his father replied. "Quite often when people think they're telling us about God, they're really telling us about themselves and their problems. Or else they're trying to explain things they don't understand. I think that's happened here."

"What do you mean?" Jack asked, looking a little confused.

"Well, it has always taken sweat and hard work to grow things in the earth," Mr. Parker explained, "and it still does. But is was especially hard for the tribes who first told these stories, because the land they lived in was often dry and rocky. Sometimes it was just about impossible to get *anything* to grow. They had to eat to stay alive, and they wanted to know *why* food was so hard to come by. So . . ."

". . . so they blamed it on God." Jack finished the sentence for his father.

"That's about it, Jack," his father replied, "but there's more to it than that. As I understand it, the man and woman in this story stand for 'Man' and 'Woman'—all men and all women. We've already seen how much they are like us, and we like them, so . . ."

". . . so they're really blaming it on themselves, aren't they?" Suzanne asked.

"I think what Daddy is saying, children," Mrs. Parker explained, "is that it's not a question of who's to blame. But, it's interesting for us to know that the people who told these stories wondered *why* snakes crawl on their stomachs, and *why* women suffer in childbirth, and *why* food is hard to grow. And, it's interesting for us to know what their answers were. We must realize, though, that often their questions and answers tell us much more about *them* than about God."

"That's right, Mary," agreed Mr. Parker. "In reading the Bible together, we have to be careful that we know when a man is telling us about people, and when God is telling us about Himself through man. It's important that we keep the two separate."

"But how do you tell which is which?" asked Suzanne.

"We have to do a little measuring," Mrs. Parker answered.

Jack looked puzzled.

"Jack," his mother said to him, "Roger is your best friend. If another boy tells you about his best friend, you can tell whether he is *really* a best friend by comparing him with Roger. Roger, then, is your yardstick for measuring friendship.

"In the same way, Jesus is our yardstick," she continued. "For us Christians, God is known most clearly in Jesus' life. When someone says to us, 'This is what God is like,' we can measure what they tell us by what Christ tells us. And then we know if this someone is really talking about God or not. You see?"

"When we measure these stories by what Jesus tells us about God," Mr. Parker concluded, "we find that in some places they fall short. Well, let's get on with our story . . ."

"Hold on a minute!" Jack interrupted. "How does this measuring work?"

"That's a fair question," Mrs. Parker said. "Let's all try a little measuring. What does the Garden of Eden story say about pain?"

"That God put it in childbirth in order to punish the woman," Suzanne answered.

"What does Jesus tell us about pain?"

"Well," Suzanne said, "He certainly didn't like sickness, because He went around making people better. I guess that sickness means pain, too."

"Yeah, that's right," Jack agreed. "He sort of treated it as though it was an enemy or something."

"And nobody would create enemies—especially God," Suzanne added.

"How does this part of the story measure up to what Jesus tells us about God?" asked Mr. Parker.

"It doesn't!" Jack replied. "Then you mean this part of the story is telling us more about man than about God, don't you?"

"Right! Let's try one more measuring job," Mrs. Parker said. "What does the story we've been reading tell us about God and the world?"

"Well," Jack began, "that He made it, and all things, and us."

"And," Suzanne added, "that He's sort of the Father of everything."

"What does Jesus say about this?"

"Jesus calls God 'Father,'" Jack said, "and I think He means Father of everything."

"He does," Mr. Parker said.

". . . so", Suzanne concluded, "this part of the story must be *really* telling us about God."

"Boy, we'd sure be in the dark—wouldn't we?" Jack said, half to himself. "I mean reading the Bible without Jesus."

"That's a pretty good way to put it, Son," Mr. Parker said. "You might say that Jesus is a kind of lamp that lights up the Bible for us. Well, let's get on with our reading."

Mr. Parker read on for a few verses, and then said,

"God now deals with Adam and Eve together . . ."

The man called his wife's name Eve, because she was the mother of all living. And the LORD God made for Adam and for his wife garments of skins, and clothed them.

. . . the LORD God sent him forth from the garden of Eden ("With Eve, of course," Mr. Parker added), to till the ground from which he was taken. He drove out the man; and at the east of the garden of Eden he placed the cherubim, and a flaming sword which turned every way, to guard the way to the tree of life.

"I'd been wondering about that . . ." Suzanne muttered.

"About what, dear?" Mrs. Parker asked.

"About why the man and woman didn't have names,"

Suzanne replied. "That was the first time in the whole story that they both had names."

"It always sounded like God was talking to some of the animals," Jack agreed. "You know, 'Come here, dog,' 'Come here, horse,' 'Come here, *man*.' I feel a lot better now that they have names. It's as though you can know them now."

" 'Adam' and 'Eve,' " Suzanne said thoughtfully. "Those are nice names. They make the man and woman sound as though they belong to something."

"Yeah," added Jack. "Kind of like they're a part of a family."

Sammy had fallen asleep in Mrs. Parker's arms. She looked down at him. Raising her eyes, she looked at Jack and Suzanne and smiled.

"I imagine that's just what names do mean."

CHAPTER SEVEN

Suzanne's Friends

"Mother, we're going upstairs."

Suzanne had just come home from school. She dropped her books on the kitchen table and grabbed two of the freshly baked cookies Mrs. Parker had spread out on brown paper to cool. She took a bite of one and gave the other to the girl who had followed her in the door.

"Here, Cathy," Suzanne said, "these are Mom's specials."

"Mmmm, are these good! Oh," Cathy said with her mouth full, "hello, Mrs. Parker."

"Hello, Cathy." Mrs. Parker smiled. "If these cookies are so good, I guess we can spare one more for each of you. Now run on upstairs and play. I'll call you when it's time for Cathy to go home for supper.

"By the way," Mrs. Parker added, "where's Marge today?"

The Parkers had been in their new home for a little over two months. In that time, Cathy, Marge, and Suzanne had become best friends. They were always together. In fact, just the other night, Mr. Parker had told Mrs. Parker he sometimes wondered whether he had one daughter or three.

So it was quite natural that Mrs. Parker was surprised when Suzanne and Cathy came home without Marge. Since she got no answer to her question except two very strange looks and some embarrassed giggles, Mrs. Parker asked it again.

"I thought I saw Marge on her way home just before you two came in to eat all my cookies." (They each had eaten two more.)

"Why didn't she come with you?"

"Don't ask me," Cathy said.

"How should *we* know what Marge does?" Suzanne

said. Then she added quickly, "And what's more, why should we care?"

"Oh excuse me. *Excuse me,* ladies! I only thought that since you were such good friends—or, at least you were yesterday. . . ."

Suzanne didn't let her mother finish.

"That was yesterday, and yesterday's not today." Suzanne turned her back to her mother, stuck her nose up in the air, and marched upstairs with Cathy following.

"There are *some* things," she called down to her mother from upstairs, "that *real* friends just don't do!"

Mrs. Parker slipped on her coat to go to the store. As she opened the door, she stopped and thought for a minute. "Oh, I don't know," she said, shrugging her shoulders, "I guess I just don't understand."

That was exactly what Mrs. Foster said to her at the store. Mrs. Foster was Marge's mother. Mrs. Parker met her at the meat counter in the supermarket.

"Mary," Mrs. Foster said, "I just don't understand—*I just don't understand!* We didn't have problems like that when we were their age, did we?"

"Oh, I suspect we did," Mrs. Parker said with a laugh. "What happened at your household this afternoon?"

Mrs. Foster told how Marge had come home from school and, the minute she got inside the door, burst into tears. She dashed upstairs—crying as though her heart would break—and slammed her bedroom door.

"I thought maybe she was sick," Mrs. Foster said, "so I ran after her to find out what the trouble was. At first, she wouldn't even let me in the room, and then, when she did, she wouldn't talk to me. I asked her why she was crying. The only thing she said—and she kept saying it—was, 'I don't know, I don't know, I don't know.'"

The butcher interrupted the conversation.

"How's this piece of roast look to you, Mrs. Foster?"

"Oh, fine—just trim off a little of the fat, will you? Now, Mary, as I was saying, then she started to moan, 'I didn't do it, I didn't do it.' I patted her on the back and she said, 'Oh Mother, I wish I were dead.'"

"Anything else, ma'am?" asked the butcher.

"A dozen frankfurters, please," Mrs. Foster said, and then continued talking with Mrs. Parker.

"Well, Mary, where was I? Oh yes—she wished she were dead. Finally, Marge sat up on the bed and said, 'I want to be alone. I *hate* them! I hate *you!* Get out! I want to be alone.'"

"That'll be $4.69," interrupted the butcher again. "Please pay the cashier at the front. Thanks, Mrs. Foster. Come again."

"Thank you, Mr. Miller. I hope it's as good as the last roast."

"Well, Mary, as I was saying," Mrs. Foster continued. "She really started shouting, and I thought I'd better get out. Whenever I get upset, I always go and buy myself a roast—you know how it is. So, here I am. I have the roast, but I don't understand. *I just don't understand.*"

"I suspect that Suzanne and Cathy are involved in this somehow," Mrs. Parker said. "I'll talk to Suzanne tonight. But don't fret about it. The amazing thing about children is that they always manage to get over these little difficulties."

Mrs. Parker walked home a little more slowly than usual, for she was not as unconcerned as she had let Mrs. Foster believe. It bothered her all during supper. She was so quiet that Mr. Parker thought she must be sick.

"Oh no, I feel fine," she assured him. "I've just been thinking. You know," she said with a laugh, "sometimes even mothers think."

As soon as supper was finished, everybody disappeared into the den to watch television, leaving Mrs. Parker with the dishes. Mrs. Parker called to Suzanne.

"Suzanne, those wrestling matches are not going to interest us girls. How about giving me a hand with the dishes? Besides, I want to talk with you."

Suzanne came back into the kitchen. She picked up a dish towel and sat on a stool, waiting for Mrs. Parker to finish clearing the table and begin washing.

"I met Mrs. Foster at the store today . . ." Mrs. Parker began but never finished.

"Oh Mother," Suzanne interrupted, "let's not go into *that*."

"Young lady," said Mrs. Parker firmly, "you just sit there on that stool and let your old mother have her say."

She proceeded to tell Suzanne of her conversation with Marge's mother. After she finished, Suzanne didn't say anything for a long time.

"Well," Suzanne said hesitantly, "we didn't mean to make her cry. But," she added quickly, "she shouldn't have told Willy."

"What did she tell Willy?" Mrs. Parker asked.

"If I told you," Suzanne said, "it wouldn't be a secret any longer—and I'd be just as bad as Marge."

"Well, secrets certainly aren't meant to be told," Mrs. Parker admitted, "but are you sure Marge told Willy?"

"Willy said she did," Suzanne replied.

"Did he tell you exactly what Marge said?" asked Mrs. Parker.

"He said Marge told him our secret—and we had promised each other that we would *never* tell," Suzanne said with a pout.

"Marge told her mother that she didn't tell him."

"Well, Willy said she did."

"Suzanne, I won't argue with you because I don't really know," said Mrs. Parker, "and I doubt whether you really know either. But I would like to tell you a story."

Mrs. Parker told Suzanne the story of a girl who had just moved into a new town where she didn't know anybody. The first day she went to school, she put on her best skirt and blouse because she thought it might help her to make new friends. When this girl came home from school that first day, she ran upstairs crying because she discovered that the girls in the new town weren't wearing that kind of skirt. "Oh Mother," this girl cried, "I was so embarrassed. Now, nobody will like me. I wish I were dead!"

"I wonder," said Mrs. Parker, "if you know who this girl was?"

"Me," said Suzanne, looking down at the floor.

"And, there's more to the story, isn't there?" continued Mrs. Parker.

"Just when this girl thought that no one in the whole world cared if she were alive or dead, the telephone rang. It was another girl in her class who—not even mentioning the embarrassing skirt—asked her over to play."

Mrs. Parker had just about finished the story.

"The girl in the story stopped crying because she had a friend. I wonder if you remember who the other girl was?" asked Mrs. Parker.

"Marge—but she still shouldn't have told our secret." Suzanne continued to look at the floor.

"It's time for you to get to your homework," Mrs. Parker said, "and then right into bed with you. Run along now—I'll finish up the dishes."

Later that evening (when they thought all three of the children were in bed fast asleep), Mr. and Mrs. Parker heard someone dialing the upstairs telephone. They both stopped reading and listened.

"Can I speak to Marge, please?" Suzanne said as quietly as she could.

CHAPTER EIGHT

Cain Gets a Mark

Mrs. Parker had never known a telephone call to be so effective.

Suzanne said nothing to her mother about the late call to Marge Foster, and Mrs. Parker did not let on that she knew the call had been made. But at breakfast the next morning, Suzanne asked if Marge could come for supper that night. Since it was Friday, and there would be no homework, Mrs. Parker said she thought that would be very nice. The misunderstanding had apparently been cleared up, and Suzanne and Marge were once again best friends.

The two girls came home from school together and played upstairs until supper was on the table, stopping only briefly to welcome Mr. Parker home from work. After supper, Suzanne and Marge chased the men into the living room and were such a help to Mrs. Parker that the table was cleared and the dishes done in record time. Mr. Parker had hardly started reading the evening paper when the whole family (and Marge) was sitting around him, waiting for Bible reading to begin.

"Holy smokes!" exclaimed Mr. Parker. "What speed demons we have in the kitchen. Jack and Suzanne, while I get the Bible, why don't you bring Marge up to date on what's happened thus far?"

The twins told Marge the Creation, the Garden of Eden, and the Adam and Eve stories. She said she knew them, but not very well. Just as Mr. Parker was about to begin reading, Mrs. Parker interrupted.

"We have only one rule for our Bible reading, Marge," she said, "and that is that anyone can ask any questions he wishes. We don't want you to be just a listener. For tonight, you are a member of our family, so this rule applies to you too. All right?"

Marge nodded her agreement, and Mr. Parker began to read.

"Just a second, Dad," Jack interrupted. "Suze and I have a couple of questions about what we were reading the other night."

"O.K., let's have them."

"We were wondering about this business of names," Suzanne said. "They're pretty important, aren't they?"

"What we mean is that, if you didn't have a name, how would you know who you were?" Jack added. "I suppose it wasn't too tough in the Garden of Eden, because Adam and Eve were the only people there. God could call, 'Man,' and Adam would know God meant him, because he was the only man around. But, when you call me for supper, if you shouted just, 'Boy'—why, that could mean anyone."

"Or, if you shouted just 'Parker,'" Suzanne broke in, "that could mean me, or Sammy, or Mommy—or even Magurk. You'd have to call, 'Jack, Jack Parker!' for us to know the person you meant. We think names are very important."

"In fact," Jack concluded, "we think that if we didn't have names, we wouldn't know to whom we belonged."

"Don't you think that is one of the meanings of Holy

Baptism?" Mrs. Parker asked. "It's in baptism that God makes our names a sign that we belong to His family."

"I don't think I ever thought of it that way before, Mary," Mr. Parker said. "Baptism does make us members of God's family, doesn't it?"

Mr. Parker didn't expect anyone to answer his question, so no one did. In fact, no one said anything for almost a minute. It was Jack who broke the silence.

"Then the names we are given in baptism are signs that we belong to God," he said. "Boy, they *are* important things."

"They sure are," agreed Mr. Parker. "Well, let's get on with our reading, shall we?"

"But, Daddy, we still have one more question," Suzanne insisted.

"Oh, I'm sorry. Let's have it."

"Well, this is harder to say," Suzanne began, "but we're surprised that Adam and Eve got their names when they did. What we mean is . . . well . . . Jack, you tell them."

"What we mean is that, if we had been God, we probably would have given them names at the beginning, but taken them away at the end. Like, when I'm friends with Willy, I always call him 'Willy.' But, when I'm not friends with Willy, I never call him by his name."

"What do you call him?" Mrs. Parker asked.

"Oh, 'Hey you,' or 'Fathead,' or names like that. It's sort of as if when people do things we don't like, we take their names away. I guess that's wrong, though, because we didn't even know what Adam and Eve's names were until they did something they shouldn't have done. It doesn't make too much sense."

"Children," Mrs. Parker said, "when would you say that a person needs love most?"

Suzanne thought about this for a minute.

"I guess when he's cross and mean . . . and lonely."

"Oh, oh," Jack muttered. "I think I'm beginning to get the pitch. A name means that someone knows us and takes care of us. When they disobeyed God, that was when Adam and Eve most needed to know they were being cared for. That was when they most needed names."

"But, to want to take care of somebody," Suzanne added, "means that you love them. So names really mean that someone loves us. Is that right?"

"That's right," Mrs. Parker replied. "Your name is 'Suzanne Parker' because Daddy and I love you, and it is as 'Suzanne Parker' that God loves you. That makes names pretty nice things, doesn't it?"

"It sure does!" Jack said. "But, if I had been God, I guess I would have done it the other way round. Wouldn't that have been awful?"

"It sure would have been, Son," Mr. Parker agreed, "but we aren't God, and things aren't switched around. We have names as signs that God loves and cares for us —and that's pretty good news!"

Mr. Parker continued reading.

Now Adam knew Eve his wife, and she conceived and bore Cain, saying, "I have gotten a man with the help of the Lord." And again, she bore his brother Abel. Now Abel was a keeper of sheep, and Cain a tiller of the ground....

"What's a 'tiller'?" Suzanne asked.

"It means 'farmer,' " her father replied. "Cain was a farmer."

Marge had been silent up to this point. Now, she spoke for the first time.

"Sounds like the beginning of a TV western," she said with a laugh. "You know, the story of a fight between the ranchers and the farmers."

"By golly, Marge," Mr. Parker said in amazement, "you haven't missed it by much. That's just what this story is—a struggle between a shepherd (a sheep ranch-er) and a farmer. Listen."

In the course of time Cain brought to the LORD an offering of the fruit of the ground, and Abel brought of the firstlings of his flock and of their fat portions. And the LORD had regard for Abel and his offering, but for Cain and his offering he had no regard. . . .

"I wonder whether the tribes who first told this were shepherds or farmers?" asked Mrs. Parker.

"I think they were wandering tribes of shepherds, Mary," her husband replied. "When they told this story, it had a happy ending for the shepherds. They worked it out so that God liked them better than the farmers. I suppose if I were a shepherd, that's the way I'd tell it."

"That's what I suspected," Mrs. Parker said thoughtfully, "but I'm really concerned about God's attitude toward their offerings. That's what this part is about, isn't it?"

Suzanne raised her hand, and then pulled it down with an embarrassed giggle.

"I thought I was in school." She blushed. "But, I think it's about offering too, Mother. And what they say about God sure doesn't sound much like Jesus."

"What do you mean, Suzanne?"

"I mean that Jesus said something about God liking any offering if it was made in the right spirit. There was

a story . . . oh yes, now I remember . . . there was a story
about a poor widow who made God happy by giving the
only penny she had, even though everybody else gave
a lot of money and expensive things. That's a lot different
from this story."

"It sure is, Suzanne," agreed Mr. Parker, "although
this story doesn't mention the spirit in which Cain made
his offering. But you've done some measuring for us, and
I think we'll have to agree that this part of the story probably tells us much more about people than it does about
God."

So Cain was very angry, and his countenance fell.
("That's his face," Mr. Parker explained.) The LORD
said to Cain, "Why are you angry, and why has your
countenance fallen? If you do well, will you not be accepted? And if you do not do well, sin is couching at
the door; its desire is for you, but you must master it."

"What's crouching at Cain's door?" Jack looked a little
bewildered.

" 'Sin,' " his father replied. "And it's 'couching'
(which means 'lying there'), not 'crouching.' "

"The story's saying that when things didn't go right
for Cain," he continued, "it was because he'd done some-

thing that had displeased God. What do you all think about that?"

"I think we need some more measuring," Mrs. Parker said. "Why, that's a terrible thought, and it gets worse later on in the Old Testament. They even said that when you were sick, it was because you had said or thought or done something that made God angry. I would find it hard to love a God like that—or to believe that He loved me. Besides, that isn't what Jesus tells us. John, let me see the Bible for a minute."

Mr. Parker handed her the Bible. The others sat back and waited while she thumbed back and forth through the New Testament.

"I can't seem to find what I'm looking for," Mrs. Parker said as she ran her finger down page after page.

"You don't really need a particular instance, do you?" asked Mr. Parker. "Isn't the fact of Jesus' life—everything about Him—the real answer? The way He cared about all kinds of people; the way He forgave? I suggest that in the Cain story we have, as Jack said last night, people both blaming themselves *and* passing the buck to God. Mother's right," Mr. Parker concluded, "the story doesn't tell us as much about God as it does about the people who told the story. Do you all agree?"

"I sure do," Jack said quickly. "Boy, if God was mad

at me every time I didn't do right, He'd be mad at me
most of the time."

Cain said to Abel his brother, "Let us go out to the
field." And when they were in the field . . .

"I'll bet he wants to say he's sorry," Marge said.
"Maybe so, Marge," Jack commented, "but if I was
Abel, I'd be mighty careful."

And when they were in the field, Cain rose up against
his brother Abel, and killed him. . . .

"What'd I tell you?" Jack whispered to Marge.

Then the LORD said to Cain, "Where is Abel your
brother?" He said, "I do not know; am I my brother's
keeper?"

"Oh my goodness!" Marge exclaimed. "He lied to
God. Isn't that terrible!"
"It certainly is, Marge," Mrs. Parker agreed. "I wonder,
though, if whenever we lie, we aren't—in a way—lying to
God?"
The others had hardly enough time to begin thinking

about that question, when Mrs. Parker asked another.

"But, are we?—our brother's keeper, I mean."

"I guess God wants us to be," answered Suzanne.

"Being *this* brother's keeper," Jack said, pointing to Sammy, "is like being put in charge of a barrelful of monkeys."

"Oh yeah!" Sammy yelled, and jumped off the couch to take a swing at his brother that missed. He stuck his tongue out at Jack and then jumped back up next to his mother. She smiled at him, then looked at Jack.

"I'm sure that's not the kind of keeper they mean,

Jack. Maybe the question should be, 'Ought I to love and care for my brothers?' What would you say to that?"

"I guess that I ought to," Jack answered, "but sometimes Sammy makes it a little bit hard."

"Oh, don't be silly," Suzanne said to Jack. "Of course Mother means us, but she means more than just our family."

"Yeah? Who, then?"

"Well, I guess . . . I guess everybody whom God loves," she replied.

"Wow! That's everybody in the whole world." Jack slapped his hand to his forehead. "What a job!"

" 'What a job!' is right," agreed Mr. Parker, "but that's the job that's given to us."

"Well, let's get this story finished," he went on. "Because of what Cain did, God curses the ground so it will be even harder for Cain (and all other farmers) to grow things. Then God tells Cain that he will never be able to live at peace anywhere in the world. Cain replies that he'll probably not be able to live at all, for people will want to kill him for murdering Abel. God then says to Cain . . ."

"Not so! If any one slays Cain, vengeance shall be taken on him sevenfold." And the LORD put a mark on

Cain, lest any who came upon him should kill him. Then Cain went away from the presence of the LORD, and dwelt in the land of Nod, east of Eden.

"Well, God did it again, didn't He?" Jack said. "Just when you think that He's not going to have anything more to do with Cain, He puts some kind of a mark on him to protect him. It still seems backward to me, but it's nice."

"I know what you mean, Jack," agreed Mrs. Parker. "This makes me think of the Garden of Eden story. Just when Adam does something really wrong, God lets him know that he's cared for—and in a special kind of way. With Adam and Eve, it was their names that showed they belonged. Here, God gives Cain a mark to show he's cared for."

Jack looked very thoughtful. He put his chin in his hands, and it was a moment before he spoke.

"It's almost as though there's a kind of agreement that God is trying to tell them about, isn't it?"

"That seems to be it, Son," Mr. Parker said. "It's as though there's an agreement God is trying to tell them about."

CHAPTER NINE

Big Brother

One day in early October, a truck had pulled up in front of the vacant lot next door to the Parker's house. Three men got out, opened up the back of the truck, and took out some three-legged instruments with telescopes on the top. The men were surveyors.

Jack remembered the day very well, because he had just completed a long forward pass to Roger, who was tackled on the five-yard line. It was first down and goal to go. Just then a man from the truck broke up the game.

"O.K., kids, the game's over," he said. "We've got work to do here."

"What kind of work?" Roger said, speaking for all of the others.

"Somebody's bought this lot," the man answered, "and we're going to build a house here. You'll have to find some place else to play football. Come on, now—clear off!"

"Can't you wait until we score this touchdown?" Jack pleaded. "It won't take very long."

"He wants to be a hero," laughed Willy.

"Willy," Jack said, clenching his fists, "someday I'm going to poke you."

"Just try it, boy, just try," challenged Willy.

"Why you . . ." Jack started for Willy. Roger stepped in front of Jack and grabbed him.

"Take it easy, Jack," Roger said. "Don't let him get you mad, because that's just what he wants to do—get you mad."

"Ha!" Willy scoffed. "Let him come and fight if he's so brave."

"Shut up, Willy, or I'll poke you one!" Roger shouted at him. "Come on gang. Let's go some place else and play."

Led by Jack and Roger, the football players walked

slowly away, grumbling to each other about the loss of their playing field.

In the weeks that followed, things really happened to the empty lot. The surveyors worked for two days— measuring in every direction and driving wooden stakes into the ground to mark off the exact size and location of the new house. Then, in came a steamshovel, dump trucks, and men with shovels and wheelbarrows. They were digging the cellar and getting ready to lay the foundation. By the end of October, the walls of the foundation were up and in place.

And then, all work on the new house stopped!

After the first week of November, not a lick of work was done. Mr. Parker, who thought that an empty foundation was a danger to the neighborhood, did some investigating. He discovered that the man who had bought the lot had fallen seriously ill and ordered all work stopped. Work on the house was not likely to begin until spring. While this was most upsetting to Mr. Parker, it was welcome news to Jack and his friends. They had discovered that a lot with an empty foundation was much more interesting than an empty lot with no foundation.

For several days after the digging of the cellar began, Jack and his friends rushed home from school to watch the steamshovel and dump trucks do their work. Then,

the boys decided to dig their own cellar—an underground hut in the woods at the end of the Parker's street.

Early the next Saturday morning, Jack, Roger, Willy, and the rest happily attacked a small clearing in the very center of the woods with shovels, pitchforks, and pick-axes. The plan was to dig one large meeting room that had passageways leading to three smaller rooms. It was all to be covered over with branches and leaves so that no one would know it was there.

After the boys had worked for almost an hour, Willy straightened up and wiped the sweat from his face with the back of his hand. He looked at the hole. It wasn't much more than ankle deep.

"We'll never get this finished," he said with disgust. "We've been working all day—and look how far we've gotten. It'll take us years. Besides, I don't know why we're working so hard to dig a hole when there's one already dug next to the Parker's house. We could use that."

"Aw, you're loafing, Willy," Roger said. "Get back to work."

They all worked for another half-hour and then stopped for lunch, agreeing to come back in a week to finish.

By the next Saturday, work had stopped on the foundation next to Jack's house. In the woods that morning,

Jack and his friends did not seem to have the same enthusiasm for digging. There seemed to be even more rocks and roots in the ground than before. The digging was harder, and soon there was more complaining than digging being done. Roger stood up and let his shovel fall to the ground.

"I've been thinking," he said. "You know, that foundation next to Jack's would make a swell place for us . . ."

"That's what I told you last week," interrupted Willy. "But no one ever listens to me."

"Oh, stop your griping," Jack said to him.

"We couldn't put a roof over the whole thing, because it's too big," Roger continued, "but we could build a small hut out of wood—maybe in one corner. What do you say?"

Everyone agreed, happy at the thought of not having to do any more digging. As they walked out of the woods, they talked about plans for the new hut. By the time they reached Jack's house, the hut had turned into a clubhouse and the gang had officially declared themselves to be the Red Raiders. They sat on the foundation, their feet dangling over the side, and talked about their new club.

"We'd have to have rules," Roger said.

"The first rule ought to be 'No Girls Allowed,' " laughed one boy.

As everyone was agreeing to this, Jack spied Sammy coming out of the back door.

"And the next rule ought to be," he said quickly, " 'No Little Kids Allowed.' "

This was agreed to with even greater enthusiasm.

Mrs. Parker couldn't remember when anything had caused more fighting and crying in the family, unless it had been the time that Jack's uncle had sent the children the baby alligator from Florida. Since Jack and his friends had organized themselves as the Red Raiders, hardly a day had gone by without his getting into a fight with Sammy, or Sammy's running into the house with tears streaming down his face.

"And, it's all because of that club," Mrs. Parker said to her husband one night, having just described a pretty hectic day to him.

"It's all because of that hole over there," corrected Mr. Parker. "Somebody ought to do something about it."

"Don't start on *that* again, John," Mrs. Parker said. She was becoming tired of her husband's frequent and long speeches on the subject of the empty foundation. "The trouble all started with that club," she repeated, "and their silly rules."

Mrs. Parker was right. It was the rules that did it.

Suzanne couldn't have cared less whether girls were

allowed in the Red Raiders or not. She wouldn't have joined the club anyway. But the rule that kept Sammy out of the club made all the difference in the world to him. Normally, he didn't care if he played with Jack or not, but now that he was forbidden to play with his brother, that's all he wanted to do. As for Jack, *not* playing with Sammy had become a matter of pride.

Put together, this spelled trouble.

". . . but, after all—he *is* your brother," Mrs. Parker said to Jack one day, concluding a long talk with him on his responsibilities toward his brother.

"I almost wish he wasn't," Jack replied.

"Oh, Jack!" his mother said. She sounded very disappointed.

"Well, maybe I don't really mean that," he admitted, "but you don't know what it's like to have a little kid tagging after you every place you go. Everyone's so worried about Sammy—nobody cares how I feel. Heck, a lot of times I can't do things with the other Raiders because I have to watch out for him. I'm just a baby sitter—and you and Daddy don't see anything wrong in that."

Jack took a deep breath and then continued, "Besides, nobody else's little brother follows us around, and I don't see why mine should."

"Maybe it's just because Sammy loves you and wants to be with you," Mrs. Parker suggested.

"Love doesn't have anything to do with it," Jack protested. "Sammy just wants to be a member of the Red Raiders, that's all." Jack started to put on his coat. "Why doesn't he play with kids his own age, anyway? I don't play with Sammy's friends, so I don't see why he has to play with mine."

"Jack, try to be more considerate of Sammy," Mrs. Parker began, "because . . ."

"Tell him to be more considerate of me," Jack said, and he ran outside to play.

Mrs. Parker shook her head slowly from side to side. *Oh, well,* she thought to herself, *I suppose things could be worse.*

Mrs. Parker was right: things could be worse. They got worse when the Raiders decided they just had to have jackets with "Red Raiders" written across the back, and discovered that they would cost almost seven dollars apiece. Seven dollars seemed to be an impossible amount of money for each boy to raise, but then Roger came up with an answer.

"If we could just get half of that money from our allowances and savings," he said to the others, "then we could raise the other half somehow."

"How are we ever going to raise fifty-six dollars?" scoffed Willy, who was pretty good at arithmetic. "I've worked it out. There are sixteen of us, and at seven dollars a jacket, that means we need one hundred and twelve dollars. If we're going to raise half, that comes to fifty-six dollars. Where do you think we're going to find that much money?"

Roger looked puzzled. Willy seemed to have convinced the other Raiders that raising fifty-six dollars was a pretty impossible task. The whole idea was about to be abandoned when Joey Johnston suggested that they could put on a movie show, because his father had a sound projector and could get some wonderful films free at his office. They could show them in his basement, he said, and sell tickets to all the kids in the neighborhood for, maybe, a quarter apiece.

"O.K., genius," Roger said to Willy, "how many tickets will we have to sell to raise that fifty-six dollars?"

"Two hundred and twenty-four," Willy replied after a moment's thought. "We'll never sell that many tickets."

"Don't be so gloomy, Willy," Jack said. "I think Joey's idea is great! We'll sell that many tickets without any trouble at all."

And they did. The movie show was held on Thanksgiving weekend, and almost two hundred and fifty tickets were sold for it. The next week, the order for the jackets was sent in: *seventeen* jackets—sixteen for the Raiders, and one for Sammy.

* * *

A jacket was ordered for Sammy for two reasons. When the final ticket sales were being counted, it was discovered that Sammy had sold thirty-five tickets— more than twice as many as anyone else. The second reason was more important: Mr. Parker told Jack that either Sammy got a jacket or there would be no Parkers in the Red Raiders.

"But, Dad," Jack protested, "I didn't *make* him sell the tickets. He wanted to."

"Now Jack, you listen to me," lectured Mr. Parker. "When the Raiders decided to have a movie show to make money, you and the other boys went into business. One of the first principles of business is that a man is rewarded for work that he does. Sammy worked for you and the other boys, and he is entitled to a reward. That reward is a jacket—and that's final!"

"Golly, how will I ever tell this to the other kids?" Jack mumbled nervously.

"You should have thought of that before you sent Sammy out peddling tickets for you," his father replied.

"Then everybody's kid brother will want a jacket," Jack said.

"That won't be any problem," Mr. Parker said. "No one else sent their younger brother out selling tickets."

Jack put his chin in his hands and pouted.

"May I make a suggestion?" Mrs. Parker had just

come in from the kitchen. "Since Jack and Sammy have been fighting about this for the past hour, it may be that Sammy will want a different jacket from the ones that the Raiders are ordering. If so, that ought to make it a little easier for Jack. Let's ask Sammy."

Mrs. Parker called Sammy down from upstairs. His eyes were still red from crying. Mrs. Parker asked him if he wanted a jacket like Jack's.

"I don't want anything like his," Sammy replied vehemently. "I want my own special jacket."

Jack heaved a sigh of relief.

Sammy and Mrs. Parker talked about Sammy's jacket, finally deciding on a blue and white one with "Sammy Parker" written across the back.

"Jack," Mr. Parker said, "if you want, I'll speak to Roger about this."

"No, I'll do it," Jack said, and left the room. Sammy climbed down off Mrs. Parker's lap and followed his brother.

Outside, Jack explained the whole thing to the Raiders, and was surprised by their reaction. They didn't seem upset at all.

"If it hadn't been for Sammy, we wouldn't be ordering any jackets," one boy commented.

"And besides," said another, "just as long as he doesn't

want 'Red Raiders' written across the back, it doesn't make any difference if he has a jacket or not."

"Well, that's settled," Roger said. "Let's go over to the foundation and play."

As the Red Raiders walked away from the Parker house, Sammy followed close behind.

"Sammy," Jack shouted at him, "you've given me enough trouble today. Get home! Go on—get out of here!"

"Yeah, runt," Willy said, giving Sammy a push that sent him sprawling, "get lost."

Jack was at Willy in a flash. Before Willy knew what happened, a right hand to the jaw knocked him flat on his back.

"Keep your hands off my brother," Jack shouted at Willy. "If anybody's going to push him around, I'll do it."

Sammy walked up to Jack and, with all his might, hit him in the stomach.

"I don't want anyone to push me around, not even you," he said angrily. Then, crying, he turned and started to walk home.

Jack looked at Sammy in surprise. Holding his jaw, Willy laughed at Jack. No one else said anything.

* * *

Jack stopped in front of Sammy's room on his way to bed that night. The door was open. He stood in the hall for a moment, and then decided to go in. From the foot of Sammy's bed, Jack looked down at his sleeping brother.

"Sometimes, I just don't understand you," Jack said half aloud. He stayed there for almost two minutes. Then, shaking his head, he turned and went into his own room.

Sammy was not aware of being watched as he slept. Except for the silent rise and fall of his chest, he lay perfectly motionless. His quiet appearance gave no hint of the active dream that was now in progress. The day that had just ended was being relived. In this dream, Sammy was talking to Jack.

"Jack," he said in his dream conversation, "sometimes I just don't understand you."

CHAPTER TEN

A Bow in the Sky

"Mary," Mr. Parker said as he handed the Bible to his wife, "since you're the expert on floods, why don't you do the reading tonight."

Just as Mr. Hall had warned them, the Parkers found that understanding the Bible took a bit of work. They had brought home some books from the parish library and each night would study about the next Bible reading.

But last night, Mr. Parker had to go to a meeting. So Mrs. Parker did the homework all by herself.

"Well, I'm not an expert," she confessed, "but I'll try —if you all will help me. Tonight we're going to read about Noah and . . ."

". . . and the flood that killed everybody. Oh boy!" Jack said enthusiastically.

". . . and about all the giraffes, and lions, and tigers, and elephants," Sammy added, clapping his hands together. He remembered the record he had played over and over and over again on his record player.

"Boy-oh-boy," Mr. Parker said, "I'll bet you didn't think you were going to get that much help, did you?"

"I certainly didn't," laughed Mrs. Parker. "Before you all leave me with nothing to say, I'd better tell you the little bit I learned doing my homework last night."

"After Cain went to live in that land with the wonderful name of Nod," she began, "he married and had a child named Enoch. And . . ."

"Hold on a second," Mr. Parker said. "If Adam and Eve were the only people around, whom did Cain marry?"

"Oh, Daddy, you're worse than Jack," Suzanne said, sounding very disgusted. "You know that's not the kind of question we're supposed to ask, because that's not the kind of thing these stories are trying to tell us."

"Thank you, Suzanne. I hope that puts him in his place." Mrs. Parker said, winking at her husband.

"Now as I was saying," she continued, "Adam and Eve had another child whom they named Seth. Between Enoch and Seth and their families, a great many children and grandchildren and great-grandchildren were born— far too many for me to remember their names, although I do remember Methuselah who was supposed to have lived nine hundred and sixty-nine years. I think he's the Bible's oldest man. He was also the grandfather of Noah."

"He's the guy I sometimes feel as old as," laughed Mr. Parker. "You know the saying, '. . . as old as Methuselah.'"

"Well, you are pretty old, Dad," agreed Jack.

"If you two are through with the aches and pains of old age, we can get on," Mrs. Parker broke in.

"According to the story, as the number of people on the earth increased, there was constant arguing and fighting and dishonesty among them. This made God unhappy about the whole situation. So, since . . ."

. . . the earth was corrupt in God's sight, and the earth was filled with violence. . . . God said to Noah, "I have determined to make an end of all flesh; for the earth is filled with violence through them; behold, I will destroy them with the earth. . . .

"My goodness, how many times I've felt like that myself," Mr. Parker commented. "You know, I get working on a job, and everything seems to go wrong. I always wish I could throw the whole thing out and start all over again. I guess that's what God feels like here."

"I've felt that way too, Dad," Jack said, "but I've never wanted to throw people away—although I would have been willing to sell Sammy cheap yesterday, when he made such a fuss about the jacket. But, I'm glad I didn't."

"I don't know who was making more fuss, you or Sammy," Mrs. Parker laughed, "but I'm glad you didn't sell him cheap—because I like having you both around. But, I agree with you, Jack, this doesn't sound much like Jesus. Yet I wonder if the story still doesn't tell us something important about God? We've been so worried about what the punishment was, that we've never even talked about *why* God punishes."

"You've lost me, Mom," Jack said.

"Me, too," agreed Suzanne.

"Well, take this story as an example," Mrs. Parker explained. "You all know that God tells Noah to build an ark—a big boat—and to put two of every animal into the ark, because He's going to destroy the world with a flood. So, this story says that the flood was God's punishment. Is that right?"

"Yes, that's right," Suzanne agreed, "but I still don't think that God would . . ."

"Slow down, girl," Mrs. Parker said, patting Suzanne's hand. "Listen to what I learned doing my homework last night. The men who study about ancient people (they're called 'archaeologists') say that the Bible is probably right when it tells us that it rained for forty days and forty nights. There was a real, honest-to-goodness flood. It seemed to cover up the whole world.

"The flood was so terrible," Mrs. Parker continued,

"that the people couldn't forget it. They talked about it constantly."

"Sort of like the way Grandpa keeps talking about the Blizzard of '88?" Jack asked.

"Just like that, Jack. Well, the story of the flood soon became one of the tales these ancient people told around their campfires, and finally it found its way into the Bible."

"Then you mean that God really did this?" Suzanne asked, a little bewildered.

"I don't think Mother's saying that," answered Mr. Parker. "Look at it this way, Suzanne. If you were blindfolded and someone slapped you in the face, would you ask any questions?"

"I certainly would," Suzanne replied. "I'd want to know *who* slapped me and *why* I was being slapped."

"Well, when the flood rolled over these people," Mr. Parker continued, "it was just like nature slapping them in the face, and they wanted answers to the same questions you just asked. They wanted to know, '*Who* did it?' and '*Why* did it happen?'"

"You see, Suzanne," Mrs. Parker said, "the flood did so much damage and destruction that these people were certain it was a punishment. '*Why* are we being punished?' they asked themselves, and searched around for reasons.

When they looked back at the time before the flood, they realized that they had not lived together as they were supposed to—there had been arguing and cheating and fighting. So, they decided that they were being punished because of the way they had been living.

"But then they said to themselves, '*Who* cares enough how we live together to punish us?' "

"I guess 'God' was the only answer they could give," Jack said.

"That was their answer, Jack. So, then they decided that it was God punishing them for not living together as they were supposed to. That's the story they told around their tribal campfires."

"But Jesus says that God isn't like that," Suzanne insisted.

"Like what?" Mr. Parker asked.

"Like the kind of person who would kill everybody."

"You're right, Suzanne," her father agreed. "God isn't that kind of person. But He is the kind of person who cares how we live together. I think that's what Mother is trying to say."

"That's just what I'm trying to say. I think that the answers these people gave are the wrong answers. God isn't a destroying God. He is a *caring* God. That's what all of the stories we've read so far tell us about Him. He's not the kind of God who would create pain or make it hard to grow things or destroy the world. But, He is the kind of God who cares. That's why man was formed in God's image, because God loves him. And that's why Cain was given a mark—because God cares."

"You know," Mr. Parker said, "I think it's sometimes a little hard for us to see this in these stories because man's so busy telling us about himself. But it's there. And if we don't see it, there's not much point in our reading them."

"When are the lions and tigers and giraffes and elephants going to get in the boat?" Sammy asked.

"They got in while we were talking, dear," Mrs. Parker said with a laugh, "and not a minute too soon, because it started to rain. Noah put his wife aboard with their three sons, Shem, Ham, and Japheth. It rained so hard that there was soon enough water for the ark to float, and it floated about for several months. The ark finally came to rest on top of some mountains called Ararat. Since Noah wasn't sure whether the waters were going down or not, he sent out some birds as . . . well, sort of as scouts. First, he sent out a raven. Then he sent a dove that returned because there was no place to rest. A second dove brought back an olive leaf, a sign that the waters were going down. A third dove didn't return."

. . . the earth was dry. Then God said to Noah, "Go forth from the ark, you and your wife, and your sons and your sons' wives with you. Bring forth with you every living thing that is with you of all flesh . . . that they may breed abundantly on the earth, and be fruitful and multiply upon the earth. . . ."

Then Noah built an altar to the LORD . . . and offered burnt offerings on the altar. And when the LORD smelled the pleasing odor, the LORD said in his heart, "I will never again curse the ground because of man, for the imagination of man's heart is evil from his youth. . . ."

Then God said to Noah and to his sons with him, "Behold, I establish my covenant with you and your descendants after you . . . that never again shall all flesh be cut off by the waters of a flood, and never again shall there be a flood to destroy the earth." And God said, "This is the sign of the covenant which I make between me and you and every living creature that is with you, for all future generations: *I set my bow in the cloud,* and it shall be a sign of the covenant between me and the earth. . . . I will look upon it and remember the everlasting covenant between God and every living creature. . . ."

"What's a 'bow'?" Jack asked.

"What's the only kind of 'bow' you see when you look at the sky?"

"A rainbow!" Jack looked surprised, then puzzled. "It's another sign, all right," he muttered, half to himself, "just like the name and the mark. But," he said aloud, "what's a . . . a 'covermint'?"

" 'Covenant' is the word, Jack," his father answered. "That's the agreement you were talking about the other night. It's a special kind of promise."

"A promise of what?"

"A promise that God will care for us, silly," Suzanne said. "What do you think we've been talking about all night?"

CHAPTER ELEVEN

A Son for Abraham

The Parkers had assembled for their family Bible reading. Jack, Suzanne, and Mrs. Parker sat on the couch, with Sammy squirming in his mother's lap. Magurk lay at their feet. He had come to count on these few minutes of peace and quiet as a chance to catch forty winks before the bedtime roughhouse began. Mr. Parker settled in his favorite chair. He had just opened the Bible to the right place when Jack said,

"About this fellow Noah, Dad. If everybody was so terrible before the flood, what was with him that he got picked to build the ark?"

"Mary, you're the specialist on Noah. What about this?"

"Let me see the Bible for a second, John." She thumbed through the Noah story, and then said, "Oh yes, here it is. The Bible says he was chosen because, 'Noah was a righteous man, blameless in his generation; Noah walked with God.' "

"He doesn't sound quite human to me," Mr. Parker said. "I don't know anyone who is 'blameless.' "

"If 'blameless' means what I think it does," agreed Jack, "I don't know anybody who isn't a little bit bad at times."

"Well, I'll tell you all a secret," Mrs. Parker said in a loud whisper, "Noah wasn't as perfect as this verse would lead you to believe. Just like the rest of us, he had his bad moments, too. In fact," she continued, "the story says that even God recognized this, because after the flood, He said to Noah, 'I will never again curse the ground because of man, for the imagination of man's heart is evil from his youth. . . .' "

"I don't think I like the sound of that," Suzanne said.

"The Church says this is the result of 'Original Sin,' "

her father told her, "and, boy, I'll tell you that when I first heard it, I didn't like the sound of it either, Suzanne."

"Oh John, how you argued with Mr. Hall about that!" Mrs. Parker buried her face in her hands. "I was so embarrassed."

"There wouldn't have been any argument if he had said what he meant at the beginning. It's so simple and obvious. Jack just said it: none of us is good all the time."

"I think there's a little more to it than that," Mrs. Parker commented, "but that's about it: we all fall short of what God intends us to be."

"But, He loves us anyway," Suzanne added quickly. "That's part of the promise—the covenant, I mean—isn't it?"

"It is, Suzanne, it is," her father said. "Now, are we finished with Noah? Then let's get into the story of Abraham . . ."

Now the LORD said to Abram, "Go from your country and your kindred and your father's house to the land that I will show you. And I will make of you a great nation, and I will bless you, and make your name great, so that you will be a blessing. I will bless those who bless you, and him who curses you I will curse; and in you all the families of the earth will be blessed."

"Boy, this Abram sounds pretty special," Jack said. "Where'd he come from all of a sudden?"

"Well, he is special, because in a way the history of the Jewish people begins with him. Now, being the kind of father who anticipates the questions his family will ask, I'll *show* you where he came from all of a sudden."

From behind his easy chair, Mr. Parker pulled out a large, thin book. Placing it on the floor in front of him, he opened it to a brightly colored map. They all gathered around. Not being satisfied to sit on the floor with the rest of the family, Magurk walked right onto the map.

"Magurk! Get off the map before you drown," Mr.

Parker said, giving him a push. "You're right in the middle of the Mediterranean Sea."

Magurk gave Mr. Parker a disgusted look and walked away. He went around in two tight circles and finally lay down—his head resting on Italy.

"Now, here's where the Bible says Abram's family came from—a city named Ur," Mr. Parker continued, pointing to a spot near the top of the Persian Gulf. "At the time of the story, the coast was further north, and Ur was almost a port city. Being located right at the mouth of the Euphrates River, it was probably a pretty busy and prosperous place.

"Abram's father wanted to take his family over here." Mr. Parker traced his finger across the Arabian Desert to the shores of the Mediterranean Sea. "But, his wife must have been reading the road map upside down, because this is where they ended up."

He pointed out Haran, which was far to the north and way off course. It was near the source of the Euphrates River.

"Now, John," pouted Mrs. Parker, "you leave Abram's mother out of this. The Bible's hard enough on women as it is, without you making it worse."

"Well, anyway," laughed Mr. Parker, "it was in Haran they settled. When, years later, God called Abram out of Haran, Abram finally made it to the place his father had set out for many years before . . ."

"Oh look, there's Jerusalem," Jack said excitedly as he pointed at the map. "That's where David fought all his wars . . ."

". . . and near where Jesus was born," Suzanne added.

"You're both right," Mr. Parker said. "The land Abram lived in was the land of David and Jesus. It was known then as the land of the Canaanites, but it soon became known as the land of Israel. The Israelites consider themselves the descendants of this man whom God called out of Haran.

"Some time after Abram and his wife Sarai came to Canaan, there was a famine, and they went down into Egypt where there was still plenty of food. Now, Abram's wife was a problem to Abram. Sarai was a very beautiful woman and Abram was afraid that an Egyptian would kill him in order to marry her. So he pretended that she was his sister. She soon caught the eye of the ruler of Egypt—the pharaoh—and he took her as his wife."

"I certainly don't understand Sarai," Mrs. Parker said. "I'd rather have stayed in Canaan and starved."

"I agree with you, Mary," her husband replied, "but, the maneuver did work out pretty well for Abram. Well, the pharaoh wanted to be nice to his new 'brother-in-law,' so he helped Abram become very wealthy. But bad things began to happen to the pharaoh. When he discovered the trick Abram had pulled on him, he blamed all his troubles on his having married another man's wife. So he told Abram and Sarai to pack up and get back to Canaan. I suspect that Abram left Egypt better off than he came to it.

"Abram's nephew, Lot, had gone into Egypt with him, and he had done well also. Once back in Canaan, they kept bumping into each other, getting into each other's hair, so to speak, and friction developed between the two of them . . ."

"Can't you just see it, Suzanne?" Jack stood up and stuck his thumbs in his belt, Western style. " 'Lot, you old sheep rustler, this country ain't big enough for the two of us . . .' "

"That's about what happened, for Abram gave Lot the choice of which half of the country he wanted to live in. Lot chose the fertile Jordan River Valley (here it is on the map). At the time, this looked like the best choice, but it didn't work out that way. Apparently Abram wasn't mad at Lot, because later on he fought a war to rescue Lot from the enemy and then helped to save Lot and his family when the city Lot lived in was destroyed."

"Boy, what an exciting life," Jack said. "They ought to make a movie out of it."

"Oh, I almost forgot," Mr. Parker continued. "Abram

had a child by a servant named Hagar, and he permitted
Sarai to drive Hagar into the wilderness to die. But God
stepped in to save her . . ."

"Well! Abram may sound like a 'special' person to
Jack," Suzanne said, sounding a bit angry, "but he doesn't
sound like a *righteous* person to me. I don't think I would
like him one bit."

"Don't you think that this is part of what the story is
saying?" Mrs. Parker asked. "I don't mean that you
wouldn't like him, but that he isn't a perfect person.
Abram did many fine things and, at times, showed real
courage. Of course, he also did things that weren't fine,
and often showed himself to be a weak person . . ."

"In fact," Mr. Parker finished for his wife, "he seems
to be a person just like us—never quite becoming all that
God intends him to be."

"Well, maybe so. But, I don't know anybody who
would do to his wife what he did," Jack protested. "And
all that business about poor Hagar. I think it's terrible."

"Hold on, boy," Mr. Parker said, holding up his hands
like a policeman stopping traffic. "Not long ago, you
were glad to call Sammy 'brother' when he was willing
to sell tickets for you. But, two days ago, you didn't know
him when he wanted a jacket. You were even willing to
'sell him cheap.' That's not much different from Abram

calling Sarai 'wife' one day and 'sister' the next. Maybe it's even worse."

"It's something we all do, Jack," Mrs. Parker said. She patted Jack's shoulder.

"When you put it that way," Jack said, "I guess you're right. Gee, I've done that sort of thing a lot of times."

"So have I," Suzanne admitted reluctantly. She added quickly, "But, none of us has done anything like sending that poor servant girl into the wilderness."

"Well, we haven't banished anyone to the woods—if that's what you mean," Mrs. Parker said, "but we've all done things just as bad. I seem to remember once when you and Cathy wouldn't play with Marge because you thought she had told your secret. Marge spent the rest of the day alone, crying in her room. There are times, you know, when your own room can be much lonelier than a wilderness."

"I think I see what you mean," Suzanne said quietly. "I guess it's just that I expected Bible people to be different from us."

"That's the trouble with most of us who read the Bible," Mr. Parker said. "We think Bible people are somehow better than other people—I guess because they're in the Bible. But they're not better. They're just people. Why! if God had waited for men to become perfect before they could do His work, He'd still be waiting.

"There was work to be done," he continued, "and Abram was chosen to do it—not because Abram was better than anybody else, but because God figured he could do the job. So God entered into covenant with Abram, and sealed it in three ways . . ."

". . . I will make my covenant between me and you, and will multiply you exceedingly." Then Abram fell on his face; and God said to him, "Behold, my covenant is with you, and you shall be the father of a multitude of nations. No longer shall your name be Abram, but your name shall be Abraham; for I have made you the father of a multitude of nations."

"The name 'Abraham' means 'father of a multitude,' " Mr. Parker explained. "Sarai had her name changed, too. From now on, she's called 'Sarah.' This was the first sign of covenant. The second sign was circumcision . . ."

And God said to Abraham, "As for you, you shall keep my covenant, you and your descendants after you throughout their generations. This is my covenant, which you shall keep. . . . Every male among you shall be circumcised. You shall be circumcised in the flesh of your foreskins, and it shall be a sign of the covenant between me and you."

"This sounds like when Cain got his mark," observed Jack. "God's really making sure this time, isn't He?"

"He sure is." Mr. Parker looked at his watch. "Hey, it's getting late, so I guess that wraps it up for tonight."

"But, Daddy," Suzanne objected. "I thought you said there were three ways God sealed the covenant with Abraham. You've only told us about two."

"Holy smokes," laughed Mr. Parker, "I've left out the most important sign. We can't stop before we cover it.

"Well, all through the story, God tells Abraham that the covenant is with him *and his children*. But the strange part about this is that Abraham and Sarah didn't have any children. And, what was worse, they were getting too old to have children. It almost seemed as though God was teasing Abraham. He would say to Abraham, 'I will make your descendants as the dust of the earth; so that if one can count the dust of the earth, your descendants also can be counted.'

"Or else," Mr. Parker continued, "God would call Abraham from his tent at night, and tell him to look up at the desert sky: 'Look toward heaven, and number the stars, if you are able to number them.' Then he said to him, 'So shall your descendants be.'

"At first, Abraham believed God, but as the years went on he began to think it was a joke. Once when God told Abraham that Sarah would bear him a son . . ."

. . . Abraham fell on his face and laughed, and said to himself, "Shall a child be born to a man who is a hundred years old?"

. . . The LORD visited Sarah as he had said, and the LORD did to Sarah as he had promised. And Sarah conceived, and bore Abraham a son in his old age at the time of which God had spoken to him. Abraham called the name of his son . . . Isaac.

"Oh, what a wonderful sign," Suzanne said.

"You know, John," Mrs. Parker said, "it's almost as though history was beginning all over again with Abraham. Maybe with the stories of Adam and Cain and Noah, the history of *people* begins. But with this story, begins the history of the *special people* God would use to show all men and women what He was really up to."

CHAPTER TWELVE

The Menace

"It's not only most unattractive, but it's a menace to the whole neighborhood."

Mr. Parker sounded very upset, and a little bit angry as well. The Parker family was at supper and, in the last few weeks, they had come to expect Mr. Parker to express his opinions on the terrible condition of the empty lot next door. It was becoming his favorite subject.

"What's a 'menace'?" Jack asked.

"That's a menace!" Mr. Parker was almost shouting. He pointed dramatically in the general direction of the empty lot.

Suzanne giggled because she thought her father looked like a district attorney on television accusing somebody of murder.

"Suzanne!" Mrs. Parker said sharply. Then she turned to her husband and said quietly, "I think Jack wanted to know what 'menace' meant."

"Excuse me, Son," apologized Mr. Parker, adding for Suzanne's benefit, "and, young lady, this is no laughing matter.

"A 'menace,'" he explained, "is something that is dangerous. Children could fall into that big hole over there and be killed. Because it's not marked by lights at night, even grownups might injure themselves. Soon we may have snow, and then it will be worse.

"When something like that is dangerous to the public," he continued, "that is, to all the people in a neighborhood, it's called a 'public menace.'"

Mrs. Parker never said much about "the menace," but she was beginning to get as upset about it as her husband. On rainy days, mud would be tracked all over the house. On clear days, the wind would blow up clouds of dust that turned the Parker's white house brown, clean windows dirty, and drying clothes dusty. Mrs. Parker never complained—she left that for her husband to do.

But the afternoon that Magurk jumped into the foundation she couldn't stand it any longed. She went right to the telephone and called her husband at his office.

". . . And then, to make matters worse, Magurk just got stuck in the foundation and I had to rescue him—and I ruined a pair of my best stockings doing it. John," she concluded, "if something isn't done about that hole soon, I think I'll go crazy."

Mr. Parker smiled at the thought of Mrs. Parker climbing in and out of the foundation, but agreed that something did have to be done.

"That's what you've been saying for almost two months now," Mrs. Parker said with a touch of bitterness. "Something has to be done *soon*."

"All right, all right." Mr. Parker replied quickly. "I'll do something tonight. I don't know what—but I'll do it."

It was a quiet supper that night—too quiet! Jack and Suzanne knew when a storm was brewing. But Sammy was too young to know. He babbled continuously about everything and nothing, and even invented a few new words when he ran out of old ones.

"Oh, Sammy—*will you* PLEASE shut up!" Jack said with disgust.

Sammy did stop talking, but he burst into tears. He scrambled down from his chair and ran from the room.

"Now look at what you've done, Jack," Mrs. Parker said with a sigh.

"What'd I do?" Jack sounded surprised. "I just told him to shut up. Jeepers—you can't say anything around here without being jumped on for nothing. For nothing!"

"That'll be enough of that kind of talk, young man." Mrs. Parker got up to go after Sammy. "You're years older than he is—old enough to know better."

In a few minutes, she returned with Sammy. She sat down at the table again and Sammy sat on her lap, his face buried in her shoulder. He refused to look at anyone.

Well, thought Mr. Parker, *now's as good a time as any.*

"Hear ye, hear ye," he proclaimed. "The Court is now in session. Stand by for the verdict of the Court."

Jack felt that he was expected to laugh. But something told him that this was not going to be very funny. So he didn't. His face had a serious look as he paid close attention to his father.

"Whereas," Mr. Parker continued, "the empty foundation next door is widely known to be a public menace and, whereas (on the testimony of Mrs. John Parker—a noble and honest woman) it has also been declared to be a public nuisance . . ." Mr. Parker paused for breath, "it is the decision of this Court that it is—from this time forward—'Off Limits' for all members of this family, including Magurk Parker.

"Disobedience," Mr. Parker added quickly, "will be met by severe punishment. *The Court has spoken!*"

"How about that father of ours," Jack said with a nervous laugh. "He's a real card—isn't he, Suze?"

"This, my good son, is no joke. You are to stay away from the lot next door. And when I say 'away,' I mean 'AWAY.'"

"Well, that decision doesn't help my problem with the dust," Mrs. Parker said, "but I guess it's a start."

"Holy smokes, Dad, you can't really mean that," Jack said anxiously. "I've got to go there. That's where our club meets. If I can't play in the foundation, I can't belong to the club—and *I've got to belong to the club,* because . . . well, because everybody does."

"Serves you right for starting such a silly club," Suzanne said, sticking out her tongue at Jack.

Mrs. Parker said, "Suzanne!" and Jack said, "You keep out of this!" at the same time.

Mr. Parker slapped his hand on the table.

"I want all of you to be quiet," he said firmly. "That foundation is a danger to our neighborhood and to this family especially (since we live next door to it). *None of you* shall go near it. And that's final!"

Having said this, Mr. Parker went into the living room to read the newspaper. The matter was closed.

Mrs. Parker sighed, and got up to give Sammy his bedtime bath. Suzanne headed for homework, but not before she stuck out her tongue at Jack once more. It was wasted on Jack, for he didn't see it. His chin rested on his hands, and he stared blankly at the wall opposite him.

"It just isn't fair," he muttered to himself. "A sissy—that's what this will make me—a sissy. Everybody else can play there. But—*oh no!*—not Jack. Daddy's afraid Jackie will hurt himself."

He hit the table hard once with his fist and then started clearing dishes. It was his turn.

Most of the club sympathized with Jack—except, of course, Willy. As Jack had come to expect, Willy was not at all sympathetic. For three days in a row, Jack and Magurk sat on the sidelines sadly watching the Red Raiders play in the foundation and suffering in silence under the steady stream of Willy's sarcasm.

Then came the fourth day.

It was a Saturday, and the Raiders had spent a good part of the morning gathering acorns. By noon they had filled several bags. After lunch they put a large basket in

the center of the foundation floor, and they sat on the top of the foundation walls throwing acorns at it. They had chosen sides and were keeping score: five points for a "basket," three points for hitting it but not staying in.

"Hey Jack," yelled Roger, "you could do this with us. Your father said you couldn't play *in* the foundation— but he didn't say anything about playing *on* it."

"I don't think I'd better," Jack said hesitantly.

"Aw, come on—he'll never know!" shouted several of the boys.

"Well," Jack said, remembering that no one was home today, "maybe just this once. How about it, Magurk?"

Magurk barked his approval, and Jack was up on the wall with the rest of them quicker than you could say "Afghanistan." The game was going along nicely when one of the boys noticed Suzanne, Cathy, and Marge standing on the sidewalk watching.

"Hey," he shouted, "no girls allowed here."

"We're not bothering your silly old game," Suzanne said. "And besides, Jack's not supposed to be there. Wait till Daddy hears about this."

"Don't snitch, Suze," pleaded Jack. "Anyway, I'm *on* the foundation, not *in* it."

Then it happened.

Somebody lobbed an acorn at the girls. Then another. And another. Suddenly, acorns were raining on them.

Cathy and Marge beat a hasty retreat, but Suzanne (despite what Jack thought about girls, and his sister in particular) was brave. Covering her face with her hands, she marched toward her attackers.

"You horrible, spiteful, nasty boys," she shouted at them. "I'll show you!"

She bent over and grabbed a huge clump of dirt which she raised over her head and threw.

"This'll teach you a lesson," she screamed at them.

It wasn't a clump of dirt she threw. The dirt covered a good-sized rock like a layer of chocolate on a peanut. It hit Roger on the head with a dull thud. He fell toward Suzanne and then rolled over on his back. Blood streamed

down his face. There was absolute silence. Suddenly, Jack jumped to Roger's side and shouted,

"You've killed him! Suzanne—*you've killed Roger.*"

Suzanne burst into tears.

* * *

Mr. Parker was informed of what had happened as soon as he arrived home. Immediately he telephoned Roger's father and, as he talked, Jack nervously paced in circles in the living room.

"Why did it have to happen to Roger?" he moaned. "He was my best friend. Why couldn't it have been someone else?" A happy thought struck him. "Why couldn't it have been Willy?"

"Jack!" Mrs. Parker said sharply. "It shouldn't have been *anybody.*"

"Well, Roger's going to be all right," Mr. Parker said as he came into the living room. "Three stitches, and he's good as new. He'll have a nice scar, though, to remember the Parkers by.

"Now," he said very seriously, "let's get down to business. Suzanne, I'll deal with you later. You're going to have to learn that you don't throw things at people—no matter what they do to you."

"Yes, Daddy," Suzanne said quietly. "I'm sorry. I'll visit him every day until he's better."

"Although I must admit," continued Mr. Parker, "the boys had no business throwing acorns at you. And as for you, Jack Parker, you'll be confined to the house for one solid week!"

"I didn't throw any acorns at them," Jack said. This was the truth, but the reason was that he had run out of ammunition.

"I don't care if you did or not," insisted Mr. Parker. "You deliberately disobeyed my orders not to play in that foundation. Now see what's happened!"

"Gee, you sound as though you think I threw the rock at Roger. Suzanne threw it—and nothing happens to her. I just sit on top of the foundation wall and you . . . you . . . you make a federal case out of it."

"It was almost—my young son—a case of life or death, and all because you disobeyed my orders. You're going to have to learn the hard way," Mr. Parker said firmly.

"I didn't throw the rock—she did!" Jack was now in tears. "Punish me for playing in the foundation if you want to. But don't make out like I threw the rock. I didn't. Roger's my best friend. It isn't fair! *It just isn't fair!*"

"We'll talk no more about it." Mr. Parker turned to his wife. "Mary, you see that my instructions are carried out."

"This is worse than Russia," Jack shouted at his father, and ran upstairs.

"For that—no television!" Mr. Parker shouted back at him.

Neither Mr. nor Mrs. Parker said anything for a long time. Finally, Mr. Parker stood up and walked to the telephone.

"I've got to call up some of the other fathers. Mr. Greene (you know, Roger's father) agreed with me that we ought to put a fence around that foundation so none of the boys can play there. We're taking up a collection to buy the wood."

Mr. Parker paused for a moment.

"I guess we should have done that a long time ago."

CHAPTER THIRTEEN

Heirs of the Promise

"Well, let's see what the dictionary has to say about that, Jack," Mr. Parker said, and went over to the bookshelf to pull out the fat book of words. When he returned to his chair, he opened it and ran his finger down a page, stopping at the word "covenant." He muttered to himself as he read the definition. Then he said to Jack,

"There are a lot of meanings given for it, but I guess the one we're interested in is this: a covenant is 'an agreement between persons or parties.' Does that help you any?"

Jack had begun the evening's Bible reading by asking what a covenant *really* was. Now that he had the dictionary's definition, he scratched his head for a few seconds and then said, "That's sort of what I thought it meant—but it doesn't help much."

"It also means that both persons or parties in this covenant are bound to do something for each other," Mr. Parker said. "For example, when I say I'll give you fifty cents for shoveling the sidewalk, we have entered into a contract or covenant. You promise to shovel the sidewalk, and I promise to pay you for it. If either of us does not keep his promise, the covenant is broken."

"Now, that's *just* what I mean," Jack said. "There are always two people in a covenant, and both of them have to do something. That's what makes the covenant in the Bible so crazy. There are two people in it, all right—but only one of them has to do anything."

"I think I know what you mean, Jack, but I'm not quite with you. Keep going!"

"Well, God and man are in a covenant. That's right, isn't it? God goes around giving out names and signs and children as His end of the bargain, but man doesn't have to do anything that I can see—except maybe give God trouble. That sounds like a crazy kind of a covenant to me."

"Oh, I don't think it's crazy, Jack," Suzanne said.

"Aw, that's because you're a girl. I'm a boy, and I think a deal is a deal. If God's got to do something, then man ought to, too."

"I must admit that it seems like a one-sided agreement to me, also," Mr. Parker said.

"Well, it doesn't to me," Mrs. Parker said firmly. "When we finished reading the Abraham story I was worried about the same thing Jack was. So I read it over again—and I don't think it's a one-sided covenant at all. Let me see the Bible for a minute, John." She opened it to the Abraham story. "You remember when God took Abraham out under the desert skies and said to him,"

"Look toward heaven, and number the stars, if you are able to number them." Then he said to him, "So shall your descendants be." And he believed the LORD; and he reckoned it to him as righteousness.

"The part that caught my attention was, 'And he believed the LORD; and he (that is, the LORD), reckoned it to him as righteousness,'" Mrs. Parker continued. "I think that this is man's end of the agreement."

"What? To believe?" Jack asked. "That doesn't seem to be much to do. As a matter of fact, that's a snap."

"Oh, is it now?" Mrs. Parker asked him. "You were so worried about what 'covenant' meant, maybe you can tell me the meaning of 'believe.'"

"That's easy," Jack replied. "It means 'to think.'"

"Oh, that's not right," Suzanne broke in. "It's much more certain than 'thinking.' When you *think* something is so, it means you're not really sure. But when you *believe* something, you're sure about it."

"What do you think it means, Suzanne?" her father asked.

"I know what it means, but I can't find the right words." Suzanne thought for a minute. "It sort of means 'to depend.'"

"That's a pretty good word, Suzanne," Mrs. Parker said. "When I was thinking about it last night, the word that came to me was 'trust.' They're almost the same, aren't they?"

"I like 'trust' better," Suzanne said.

"I don't know what you're all talking about," said Jack.

"Well, Jack, when most of us think about *righteous* people, we think of people who always do the right things and never do the wrong things. But as we said the other night, we don't know any people like that . . ."

". . . and neither did God," Suzanne added. "Just as Daddy said, if God had to wait for a man like that to come along, He'd still be waiting."

"That's right, Suzanne. So, perhaps that isn't what 'righteousness' means at all. 'Righteousness' is not so much concerned with 'doing' or 'not doing' things—but it is very much concerned with *believing*. And, if 'believing' means 'trusting,' then 'righteousness' has to do with *trusting*. In the story of Abraham, it is when he trusts God that he is righteous. And his unrighteousness is seen at those times when he refuses to trust . . ."

"For example," interrupted Jack, "for example! When didn't Abraham trust God?"

"Well, God had led Abraham and his family to the land of Canaan and cared for them all that time," Mrs. Parker said, "yet Abraham wouldn't trust God to care for them during the famine, so he went into Egypt. In

Egypt, Abraham didn't trust God to continue to protect Sarah and himself, so he lied and told everyone she was his sister.

"The greatest lack of trust, of course, had to do with the birth of Isaac," Mrs. Parker went on. "From the minute Abraham entered the land of Canaan, God told him that he and Sarah would have descendants. For a while, Abraham trusted God about this, but as time passed, he didn't. It was when he stopped trusting God that he took matters into his own hands and had a child by Hagar, his wife's maid. Isn't this what he really said: 'I don't trust God to keep His promise, so I better do the best I can all by myself'?"

"I think that's what happened," agreed Suzanne, "and I think it was terrible. I don't have any trouble seeing all the bad things. I just don't see where Abraham trusted God at *all*."

"Well it certainly must have taken a great deal of trust for Abraham to leave his home in Haran to go into a strange and unfriendly land," Mrs. Parker said. "He also trusted God when he gave Lot the choice of whichever half of Canaan he wanted, and Lot chose the rich and fertile Jordan Valley. And, of course, there were some real moments of trust when God told him about the child who was to be born to Sarah . . ."

"... and there were other times when Abraham trusted God," interrupted Mr. Parker, "but the greatest example is in a story we haven't read yet. I think we might read it right now, since it describes the kind of trust Mother has been talking about. It's a short story, so let's read it straight through ..."

After these things God tested Abraham, and said to him, "Abraham!" And he said, "Here am I." He said, "Take your son, your only son Isaac, whom you love, and go to the land of Moriah, and offer him there as a burnt offering upon one of the mountains of which I shall tell you." So Abraham rose early in the morning, saddled his ass, and took two of his young men with him, and his son Isaac; and he cut the wood for the burnt offering, and arose and went to the place of which God had told him. On the third day Abraham lifted up his eyes and saw the place afar off. Then Abraham said to his young men, "Stay here with the ass; I and the lad will go yonder and worship, and come again to you." And Abraham took the wood of the burnt offering, and laid it on Isaac his son; and he took in his hand the fire and the knife. So they went both of them together. And Isaac said to his father Abraham, "My father!" And he said, "Here am I, my son." He said, "Behold, the fire and the wood; but where is the lamb for a burnt offering?" Abraham said, "God will provide himself the lamb for a burnt offering, my son." So they went both of them together.

When they came to the place of which God had told him, Abraham built an altar there, and laid the wood in order, and bound Isaac his son, and laid him on the altar, upon the wood. Then Abraham put forth his hand, and took the knife to slay his son. But the angel of the LORD called to him from heaven, and said, "Abraham, Abraham!" And he said, "Here am I." He said, "Do not lay your hand on the lad or do anything to him; for now I know that you fear God, seeing you have not withheld your son, your only son, from me." And Abraham lifted up his eyes and looked, and behold, behind him was a ram, caught in a thicket by his horns; and Abraham went and took the ram, and offered it up as a burnt offering instead of his son. So Abraham called the name of that place The Lord will provide; as it is said to this day, "On the mount of the LORD it shall be provided."

"I suppose that there are a lot of things we could say about this story," Mr. Parker commented after a moment, "but until Mother started talking about 'trust,' it certainly didn't make much sense to me. When you read it as an example of 'trust,' the fog begins to lift."

Mr. Parker leaned forward and stared intently at his three children.

"Just think," he said, sounding very amazed, "his only son! No man ever trusted that much."

"I guess I would have tried out the sacrifice routine on Ishmael first, if I had been Abraham," Jack said. "He wasn't important the way Isaac was."

"Then you wouldn't have been really trusting, would you?" his mother asked. "I think the story is telling us that it's not hard to give unimportant things in trust. But then, that's not really trust, because we don't care what happens to unimportant things. Only when we trust God in big things—things that we *really* care about—do we really trust at all.

"Jesus says that only when we offer all that we are to God—and our lives are pretty important—do we really know what life is. He's talking about trust, too. For Abraham, Isaac was dearer to him than his own life. In trust, he was offering the most important thing he possessed. And, to Abraham, this trust was counted as righteousness."

"It's hard to realize that this is 'righteousness'—just trusting," Mr. Parker said. "I'm so used to thinking of righteousness as *doing* things . . ."

"But, you still have to do things to please God, don't you?" Jack asked.

"You can't *do* anything to please God, Jack, except trust," Mrs. Parker answered, "and *doing* things will never bring us to the point of trusting. It will only lead us to do more and more things. But, if we begin with trust, we can't help but do the things that are pleasing to God and right for each other. I know it seems backward, but I think that's the way it works."

"Mother," Jack said, shaking his head, "you can lose me faster than almost anybody I know. I haven't any idea what you're talking about."

"Jack, let's us men wrestle with it for a minute," his father said. "Suppose you only liked me because of things I did for you—brought you presents every night when I came home, took you to ball games every Saturday, and scratched your back every night before you went to sleep. And suppose I knew that this was the only reason you liked me—because of the things I did for you. What would be the only way I could keep you liking me?"

"Keep doing things for me, I guess."

"Not only that," his father added, "but I'd have to

keep doing bigger and better things for you, because I'd be afraid that doing the same things wouldn't be enough. All the time this would be going on, down deep inside me I'd know that you would never come to like me just because I'm me. So, my doing things would never bring you to like, love, or trust me, would it?"

"No, I guess not."

"But, suppose that you and I begin in love and trust. You know, we like each other just because you're you and I'm me—and for no other reason. Then I can bring you presents, or take you to a ball game, or scratch your back —not to *make* you like me, but because I am already loved and trusted by you, and it's fun to do things for people you love.

"Or, I can do nothing—just be me," Mr. Parker continued, "and the love and trust is still there . . ."

"Or, John, you can even do the wrong thing," Mrs. Parker added, "and Jack would still love and trust you, even though he might be disappointed."

"And, with us, Dad," Jack said, "this works the other way round, doesn't it?"

Mr. Parker had just started to nod his head when Suzanne, who hadn't been listening too closely (because she thought she had understood her mother the first time), said, "I feel a lot better about Abraham now."

"Yeah, so do I," Jack agreed, "but don't forget all those times that he didn't trust."

"Oh, they don't count any more," she replied. "Not after what he did in this story."

"There's where you're wrong, dear," Mrs. Parker said. "They still count very much. God wants Abraham to trust Him all the time and in all things, and He is not pleased when Abraham doesn't. But the kind of covenant God offers to Abraham is one in which God always keeps His end of the bargain—even when Abraham fails to hold up his. It's the same kind He offers to us."

"Well, we're right back where we started," Jack said with disgust. "What a crazy covenant! Whoever heard of one like that?"

"I did," his father answered. "I hope I'm living in that kind of a relationship of trust right now. Isn't that what binds our family together?"

"I would hope so, John," his wife said. "Certainly this is what we want for our family—a trust that is not broken when any one of us falls short of what we can be."

"*And,* Jack, my boy," Mr. Parker said, "don't think that this doesn't take work!"

"I guess I am pretty hard to get along with sometimes —like yesterday . . ."

"Hey, I'm not talking about you," laughed Mr. Parker,

who had reduced Jack's television ban from a week to two days—and agreed not to watch television for two days himself. "I don't have half as hard a time with you as I do with myself. I'm the guy who gives you all a bad time."

"John, that's not so," his wife said. "You're no trouble at all. I'm more of a problem than . . ."

"Oh, Mother, don't be silly," Suzanne interrupted. "You're just trying to cover up for me . . ."

"Well, Sammy's the only one left," Jack said. "He's no trouble when he's asleep, and he's asleep now."

Sammy sat straight up in Mrs. Parker's lap.

"I'm not asleep, and I'm as much trouble as anybody."

The whole family laughed at Sammy's contribution. In fact, they laughed so hard that even Sammy began to think it was funny.

"You know," Jack said, "we learn something about this covenant business every night, don't we?"

"I hope we do, Son," his father agreed. "Abraham's taught us that the covenant is a two-way proposition, and that our end of the bargain is trust . . ."

". . . and that trusting isn't easy," Jack added.

Mr. Parker closed the Bible and everyone started to get up. Everyone, that is, except Suzanne. She leaned back on the sofa with her eyes closed.

"Mother," she said quietly, "you can't trust unless you love, can you?"

"I don't think you can, Suzanne."

"Then, 'believing' is more than 'trusting.' I mean, it's 'loving'—and that's the kind of covenant it is, isn't it?"

"That's the kind of covenant it is," her mother agreed. "A covenant of love."

CHAPTER FOURTEEN

God's Bad Boy

It wasn't until the New Year began that the Parkers returned to the Book of Genesis for their Bible readings. In the days before Christmas, they read the Gospel accounts of Jesus' birth instead of the Old Testament stories they had been reading since the beginning of Advent. Between Christmas and New Year's Day, they read the Prayer Book Gospels for the feast days that follow Christmas. And one night they didn't read the Bible at all, but played "Amahl and the Night Visitors" on the portable phonograph that had been one of Suzanne and Jack's Christmas presents.

The evening of January second was spent reviewing the Genesis stories they had already covered. Then, two nights were given over to the story of Isaac. The next evening, Mr. and Mrs. Parker and Sammy were ready to begin the story of Jacob, but Jack and Suzanne were continuing an argument from the night before. The argument was about the story of Isaac and how a wife was found for him.

Because he didn't want his son to marry a Canaanite woman, Abraham sent a faithful servant to find a wife for Isaac in Abraham's home country. The servant stopped his caravan of camels outside the city of Nahor. There, by a well, he met Rebekah. She gave him a drink from her water jar, watered his camels, and then invited him to stay that night at her father's house. Impressed by her kindness, the servant determined that she would become Isaac's wife. And, she did.

The Parkers agreed that the story had not added much to their understanding of God or His covenant, although they had also agreed that it was a lovely tale. All, that is, except Jack. And he made sure that everyone knew just exactly how he felt.

"I don't think God is interested in 'smoochy' love stories," Jack said to his sister.

"It wasn't a 'smoochy' love story," she replied hotly. "It

was beautiful, just beautiful. I can just see Abraham's servant meeting Rebekah at the well . . ."

"Oh brother! Just like a girl," Jack said disgustedly. "I'll bet Suze is going to spend all next week standing by the outside water faucet waiting for someone to come along and marry her."

"Mother," Suzanne whined, "say something to Jack. He's too fresh for his own good." She turned to her brother, "It was beautiful, and if you'd stop liking all those horrible things—floods and fights and murders—you'd know it was beautiful, too."

"God doesn't like love stories like that, does He, Dad?" Jack asked.

"He does too, doesn't He, Mother?" Suzanne shouted.

"Hey! Wait a second, you two," Mr. Parker said. "You're both doing what the people who wrote these stories often do. Jack's saying, 'I am not interested in love stories and, if *I'm* not interested, then *God* certainly isn't.' And, Suzanne, you're saying just the opposite: '*I'm* interested in love stories and, therefore, *God* must be, too.'

"Boy, I sure feel sorry for God," Mr. Parker concluded, "what with everyone telling Him what He ought to be like."

"Of course, John," Mrs. Parker said, "we grownups do the same thing. I mean, we expect God to want the same

things we want. That's strange, because it's supposed to be the other way round: we're supposed to want the things God wants."

"Mother's hit the nail on the head, gang," Mr. Parker said. "I guess we're so busy thinking about ourselves that we don't take the time to ask what God's got in mind for us.

"But," he continued, "getting back to the Parker twins and their problem. When Jack asked me to stick up for him, and Suzanne wanted Mother to defend her, you reminded me of the twins we're going to read about to-night."

"Which twins?" Jack and Suzanne shouted in unison.

"Jacob and Esau," Mr. Parker answered. "They were the children of Isaac and Rebekah, and the Bible says, 'Isaac loved Esau . . . but Rebekah loved Jacob.' "

"There's going to be none of this kind of favoritism around our house," Mrs. Parker said firmly. "We have three children, and we love them all the same amount— which is 'very much.' That's the way it is, and that's the way it's going to stay!"

"Well, all the trouble in this story begins partly because each parent had a favorite . . ."

"Golly, what happened?" Suzanne asked eagerly.

It was obvious that Jack and Suzanne had forgotten all

about their argument, so Mr. Parker began the story of Jacob and Esau.

"Despite the fact that they were twins, these two boys were complete opposites. Jacob was smooth skinned, but Esau's body was covered with hair. Jacob was sly and crafty, but Esau was straightforward and easily deceived. Jacob liked to stay around home, probably helping Rebekah, but Esau was a hunter and liked roaming through the hills. As I've said, each parent picked a favorite: Rebekah loved Jacob, and Isaac loved Esau.

"But, most important to the story, Esau was the twin born first. Suzanne, just the way you are a few minutes older than Jack," her father explained. "The first-born son in a family always received the father's blessing, which meant that he became the head of the family when the father died. This gave the first-born many privileges, but also the responsibility of caring for the family fell on his shoulders. It was, as you can see, a very important thing.

"Since this was the family that had received all the promises God made to Abraham, this 'birthright' (as they called it) was even more important than usual. Esau was next in line to receive it, and that was exactly how his father wanted it to be. But Jacob and Rebekah had other ideas . . ."

Once when Jacob was boiling pottage, Esau came in from the field, and he was famished. And Esau said to Jacob, "Let me eat some of that red pottage, for I am famished!" . . . Jacob said, "First sell me your birthright." Esau said, "I am about to die; of what use is a birthright to me?" Jacob said, "Swear to me first." So he swore to him, and sold his birthright to Jacob. Then Jacob gave Esau bread and pottage of lentils, and he ate and drank, and rose and went his way.

"Boy," Jack said, "either Esau didn't care about that birthright, or else he was really hungry."

"How many times have you come in from playing and told me that you were so hungry you were going to die right on the spot?" Mrs. Parker said to him. "Suppose you really were? I guess you'd give almost anything for a bit of food."

"Besides, Esau must have been so hungry that he didn't know what he was doing," Mr. Parker said, "because later on in the story, he acts as if it had never happened."

"Gee, that was a pretty dirty trick to pull on his brother," Suzanne said. "Bible people don't seem to be getting any better, do they? This is the first thing we've heard about Jacob, and already he sounds worse than the others."

"Oh, I don't think it's a matter of people getting better or worse, Suzanne," her father said. "The thing to remember is that they're people just like us—a combination of both good and bad.

"I can't help but feel that Jacob would be a mighty interesting person to know, even though you'd have to be a little wary of him. But, if you think taking Esau's birthright from him was terrible, wait till you hear what he does later. Jacob's got things up his sleeve that . . . well, for example, take the trick he pulls on Isaac to get his blessing . . ."

"When Isaac was old and his eyes were dim so that he could not see, he called Esau his older son, and said to him, "My son"; and he answered, "Here I am." He said, "Behold, I am old; I do not know the day of my death. Now then, take your weapons, your quiver and your bow, and go out to the field, and hunt game for me, and prepare for me savory food, such as I love, and bring it to me that I may eat; that I may bless you before I die."

"But Rebekah was listening outside the tent," Mr. Parker said, "and she heard everything. Now, of course, she wanted Jacob to receive Isaac's blessing instead of

Esau. So she formed a plan. She told Jacob to bring her two juicy and tender kids from their herd of goats, and she cooked up Isaac's favorite dish. Then she told Jacob that he should disguise himself as Esau, give Isaac the food, and receive the blessing. What with Isaac's bad eyesight, she thought they could pull it off.

"But, as we've said, Jacob was no dummy. He told his mother that it wouldn't work because, even if Isaac couldn't see, he could still feel and smell. Esau smelled of the animals he hunted and, more important, he was hairy and Jacob was smooth skinned. If Isaac felt him, Jacob told his mother, he would know that he was being deceived and would curse him instead of blessing him. But Rebekah had that worked out, too. She planned to dress Jacob in Esau's clothes, and then cover his smooth skin with goatskin, so that Isaac would never know the difference.

"Apparently Jacob thought that was a pretty good idea, because they tried it out . . ."

So he went in to his father, and said, "My father"; and he said, "Here I am; who are you, my son?" Jacob said to his father, "I am Esau your first-born. I have done as you told me; now sit up and eat of my game, that you may bless me." But Isaac said to his son, "How is it that you have found it so quickly, my son?" He answered, "Because the LORD your God granted me success." Then Isaac said to Jacob, "Come near, that I may feel you, my son, to know whether you are really my son Esau or not." So Jacob went near to Isaac his father, who felt him and said, "The voice is Jacob's voice, but the hands are the hands of Esau." . . . He said, "Are you really my son Esau?" He answered, "I am." Then he said, "Bring it to me, that I may eat of my son's game and bless you." So he brought it to him, and he ate; and he brought him wine, and he drank. Then his father Isaac said to him, "Come near and kiss me, my son." So he came near and kissed him; and he smelled the smell of his garments, and blessed him. . . .

"And so, Isaac gave to Jacob the blessing that had been given to him by his father Abraham," Mr. Parker said.

"Where was Esau all this time?" Jack asked.

"He was out hunting," his father explained, "and when he returned, he prepared the food as Isaac had instructed him. He brought the food to Isaac, and it was then that the deception was discovered. Isaac trembled violently when he learned of it, and Esau said to him . . ."

"Bless me, even me also, O my father!" But he said, "Your brother came with guile, and he has taken away your blessing." . . . Then he said, "Have you not reserved a blessing for me?" Isaac answered Esau, "Behold, I have made him your lord, and all his brothers I have given to him for servants, and with grain and wine I have sustained him. What then can I do for you, my son?" Esau said to his father, "Have you but one blessing, my father? Bless me, even me also, O my father." And Esau lifted up his voice and wept. . . .

"Esau did receive a blessing from Isaac," Mr. Parker explained, "but it was not the one he wanted. That had been given to Jacob."

"I feel so sorry for Esau," Suzanne sympathized.

"I do too, Suze," Jack agreed. "If I had been Esau, I sure would have been sore at Jacob."

"Esau was angry, Jack," his father said. "In fact, he planned to kill his brother. When Rebekah got wind of this, she told Jacob that he had better go into hiding before Esau caught up with him. Jacob agreed, and they planned that he should go to Rebekah's home in Haran to lie low until his brother cooled off. But, being practically the head of the family now, Jacob could not leave without Isaac's consent. So Rebekah had to pull a few more strings.

"Rebekah told Isaac that the Canaanite women were driving her crazy," Mr. Parker continued, "and that if

Jacob married one of them it would make her life miserable. I guess Isaac remembered how his father had sent to Haran for Rebekah, because he ordered Jacob to go there to find a wife. So the two schemers—Rebekah and Jacob—were again successful, and soon Jacob was safely out of Esau's reach.

"On his way to Haran, however an amazing thing happened."

. . . he came to a certain place, and stayed there that night, because the sun had set. Taking one of the stones of the place, he put it under his head and lay down in that place to sleep. And he dreamed that there was a ladder set up on the earth, and the top of it reached to heaven; and behold, the angels of God were ascending and descending on it! And behold, the Lord stood above it and said, "I am the Lord, the God of Abraham your father and the God of Isaac; the land on which you lie I will give to you and to your descendents; and your descendents shall be like the dust of the earth, and you shall spread abroad to the west and to the east and to the north and to the south; and by you and your descendents shall all the families of the earth be blessed. Behold, I am with you and will keep you wherever you go, and will bring you back to this land; for I will not leave you until I have done that of which I have spoken to you."

"And so, the covenant pops up again," Mr. Parker concluded. "God has repeated His promises to both the son and the grandson of Abraham—first to Isaac, then to Jacob . . ."

". . . who didn't deserve it," Jack finished for him.

"Well, you're right," his father admitted, but then he asked quickly, "Which one of them did deserve it?"

"I guess none of them, really," Jack admitted, "but Jacob sure seems to be the worst of the bunch."

"Later on in the story, Jack, we'll see that Jacob had his good points, too—just as Abraham and Isaac had theirs." Mr. Parker was silent for a moment. "But, it's interesting that the writers of these stories don't seem to be as anxious to cover up Jacob's defects as they were with Abraham and Isaac. I wonder why?"

For a moment, no one said anything.

"I'll take a guess, John," Mrs. Parker said. "Near the end of Jacob's life, you know, he and his family go to live in Egypt, leaving the land of Canaan that God had given them. When they do this, everything is set for Moses to lead them out. So, in a very real sense, the history of Israel begins with Jacob and his family. The writers know this, and I think they're trying to say just what Jack told us a few seconds ago . . ."

"Who? Me?" Jack asked, sounding very surprised. "What did I say?"

"You said that Jacob didn't *deserve* the covenant—and he didn't! But, you know, later in his life Jacob gets another name—*Israel*. I think these writers are trying to say that Israel—not just Jacob, but the *people* chosen by God—did not deserve all that God was doing for them. Our story tonight is trying to make this point very clear."

"Well, it's sure convinced me," Jack said.

"But, it's not just Jacob—or even all the people of Israel," Suzanne protested. *"Nobody* deserves all the wonderful things God does for them."

"Isn't this what we were saying when we read about Abraham?" Mr. Parker reminded his family. "This whole business of the covenant is not a matter of *doing* things to earn it, but of *trusting*—and not in ourselves, but in God."

"I suppose that if we deserve anything," Mrs. Parker added, "it's . . ."

". . . getting clobbered," Jack finished for her.

"But that isn't what happens," Suzanne said earnestly. "The Jacob story says that almost no matter what we do, God sticks to His end of the covenant."

"Is this the same agreement . . . I mean, the *new* covenant that Jesus tells about?" Jack asked his mother.

"The same one, Jack," she replied. "But, in Jesus, God
tells us of the covenant face to face. There we see clearly
how faithful God is in keeping His promises, and how
little we deserve His faithfulness."

"Boy, that sure sounds like good news to me," Mr.
Parker observed. "It's never news to get something you
have earned and expect, but it is *good* news to receive
something you're sure you don't deserve."

"Then the covenant is . . . well, sort of a present, isn't
it?" Suzanne asked.

"That's what it is, Suzanne," her mother replied. "It's
a gift—from God to us."

CHAPTER FIFTEEN

Suzanne Learns About Love

"Suzanne, I do wish you would come with us," Mr. Parker said. "You know it's hard to be a family unless we are all together."

"I don't care. I can't go to church any more. *I just can't!*"

"Aw come on, Suze," Jack said, sounding very disgusted with his sister. "The teacher and everybody always wants to know why you're not there—and I never know what to tell them. It's embarrassing."

"You can tell them . . ." Suzanne began to sniffle. "You can tell them that I . . . I hate God, and that I'm never going to church again!"

Suzanne couldn't hold back the tears any longer. Crying, she ran upstairs and slammed her door. Mr. Parker started to go up after her, but was held back by Mrs. Parker, who put her hand gently on his arm.

"John," she said to him softly, "I think she needs to be alone. Let's go to church, and I'll talk with her again when we come back."

Mr. Parker shrugged his shoulders, as though things were happening that he didn't understand. He put on his topcoat. While he and Jack went to get the car, Mrs. Parker bundled Sammy into his snowsuit. As they left to join the others, Mrs. Parker turned to Magurk.

" 'By, Magurk," she said. "Take good care of our little girl until we get back."

Magurk cocked his head at Mrs. Parker. As soon as the front door closed, he trotted upstairs to Suzanne. Finding the door to her room closed, he scratched at it with his paw until Suzanne let him in.

"Oh, Magurk," she moaned, "I'm so unhappy."

Suzanne pulled Magurk up on the bed and, weeping, threw her arms around him. Her sobbing finally stopped and she fell asleep, holding Magurk tightly.

It had been like this for three weeks.

Suzanne would break into tears for apparently no reason at all, and she hardly ever laughed any more. She went to school but came home as soon as classes were over. Her teacher had called Mrs. Parker to say that Suzanne refused to join in any activities with the other students, and what should she do. Mrs. Parker asked the teacher to be patient with Suzanne, as she would probably be all right in a few days.

Suzanne had been this way since the day Marge Foster was killed.

When Suzanne had refused to sing with the children's choir for Marge's funeral service, Mrs. Foster had stopped around to see her.

"Marge would have wanted you to sing with the choir, Suzanne," Mrs. Foster said. "After all, you were her best friend. I know you're unhappy, but we're all sad and unhappy. We just have to go on believing that God is taking good care of her now. If we believe that . . ."

Suzanne had listened to Mrs. Foster in silence. But when she said that "God was taking care" of Marge, Suzanne leaped to her feet.

"Why wasn't He taking care of her when she ran in front of that car?" she shouted. "No, I won't sing, I won't sing! I'm not ever going to church again."

With that, Suzanne ran from the room. Mrs. Foster

watched her go, and then rose slowly. She wiped her eyes with a damp handkerchief and started to go back to her home in which a little girl no longer played.

Not only did Suzanne refuse to sing with the choir, but she hadn't been to church since. The afternoon that Mr. Hall called to talk with her, she locked herself up in her room and refused to speak to him. For weeks, Mrs. Parker tried almost every day to talk about Marge with her daughter, but without success.

* * *

Magurk sat up as he heard the Parker car turn into the driveway. He licked Suzanne's face. She woke up, still holding on to him. He wanted to run downstairs and greet the family, but she wouldn't let him go.

"Stay with me, Magurk," she said. Suzanne thought for a moment and then buried her face in Magurk's neck. "How can they love anyone who lets such terrible things happen to His family? Maybe *they* can—but *I* can't."

Dinner that Sunday was like every other meal since the accident. Suzanne sat down at the table with the rest of the family, but for all she ate, she might just as well have stayed in her room. She picked at her food and, before dessert was served, asked to be excused.

"Not today, Suzanne," Mrs. Parker said gently. "You sit here with us until we finish."

"But I don't want to," Suzanne said.

"John, will you and Jack please clear the table and do the dishes today?" Mrs. Parker asked, ignoring Suzanne. "Suzanne and I are going for a short ride in the car."

"Oh, Mother . . ." complained Suzanne.

"Oh, yes we are," Mrs. Parker said firmly.

And they did.

They drove out into the country, turning down a dirt road that led to a bluff overlooking the river valley. Mrs. Parker stopped the car and turned off the motor. For a long time they both looked at the beautiful winter scene before them. Then Mrs. Parker spoke.

"Darling," she said, "I know how badly Marge's death hurt you—and for me to say that it hurts me, too, doesn't help much, does it?"

"No," Suzanne said, almost whispering the word.

Both mother and daughter stared blankly out the window. Suzanne began to fidget with her hands. Again, it was Mrs. Parker who broke the silence.

"Suzanne, have you ever thought much about love?"

"Well, I . . . uh . . ." Suzanne stammered. "No, I guess I haven't."

"There's no reason why you *should* have, I guess, since I didn't think much about it until I met your father. But I learned about it late—and I wanted you to learn early,

because we meet so many people all through our lives who need our love."

"Mother," Suzanne said, "I don't think I understand."

"People want many things for their children—money, success, education—but, from the first time I held you in my arms as a baby, all I wanted for you was love. I didn't learn what love was until it was almost too late—and I wanted it to be the first thing you knew. I didn't want you to know *anything* or *anybody* apart from love.

"I remember when you were four and a half (you probably don't remember); you climbed into my lap and said, 'Mommy, if you and Daddy didn't love me—I don't think I would be alive.' I thought then that you knew. But now, I'm not so sure. I'm not so sure."

Mrs. Parker's eyes filled with tears.

"I thought you were going to talk to me about Marge," Suzanne said. "I don't see what this has to do with her . . . her accident."

"The funny thing, my sweet, is that this has *everything* to do with Marge." Mrs. Parker hesitated. "Do you know what is the hardest part of loving someone?"

"Oh, I don't know . . . I guess . . ." Suzanne thought for a minute. "Maybe living *with* people? Sometimes it's awfully hard to live with Jack—and I love *him*."

"Sometimes it *is* hard to live with people you love, dear, but the hardest part of loving is living *without* the people you love." Mrs. Parker looked right at Suzanne. "I wonder if you know how hard it is to say good-by to Daddy when he goes on a business trip, or to see you and Jack go off to camp, or to take Grandma and Grandpa to the train after a long visit?

"But, then, of course you do know," Mrs. Parker said with a smile, "because you love them too."

"When Jack and I go to camp," Suzanne said, swallowing hard, "it isn't easy for us to leave you either. We've talked about it."

"Of course it isn't easy, because love works both ways." Mrs. Parker looked out on the valley below them. "Sometimes I think how hard it will be when you all go off to college. (Four years is a long time, isn't it?) And how hard it will be when you all get married and go to heavens-knows-where to live.

"It's easy to love you all when you're right here with us," she continued, "but when you're separated from us, then is when it gets hard."

"I don't want to sound like a four-and-a-half-year-old," Suzanne said, "but when Jack and I are away from you, the only way we *do* know you're alive is when we are sure that you love us and we love you. I guess you could say . . ." Suzanne thought for a moment, "I guess you could say that you're only alive when you love someone."

"I think that's probably right, Suzanne," Mrs. Parker said.

"And," Suzanne continued, sounding very serious, "if it's hard to be away from people you love . . . WHY! without love it would be impossible—we'd all be dead, or as good as dead."

Suddenly, Suzanne frowned. She clenched her fists tightly and turned to her mother.

"But what about Marge? She *is* dead—I mean, *really*."

"Oh, my," Mrs. Parker said thoughtfully, "you ought to talk with Mr. Hall about that—that's a minister's field. But I will tell you what I believe, if you want me to."

"I . . . I do want you to."

"I believe that God is love, and that He loves the world —I mean the *whole* world. And, you know Suzanne, when I think how your daddy and I suffer for the few people who are given to us to love, I can't even begin to imagine how God must feel because He has everybody to love. Do you know what I mean?"

"I'm not sure," answered Suzanne.

"Well, when you hurt yourself or are unhappy, Daddy

and I are hurt and unhappy too—because we love you. And because God loves you, He knows your hurt and unhappiness too. But think of all the hurts and unhappiness He has to bear. Well, for example, like the hurt of Marge's accident."

Suzanne turned her head quickly to look at her mother.

"God doesn't want His children hurt," Mrs. Parker said, "any more than I want my children hurt. When they are hurt, He feels it as much as I do—except He's got the hurts of all His children to feel, and I have so few."

"Do you mean that God didn't want Marge to have an accident?"

"That is just what I mean. And more than that, just as your daddy and I take care of you when you are hurt, in the same way God takes care of His children when they are hurt. That's what Mrs. Foster meant the other day."

"You know, when you say that 'God takes care of' Marge the way that you and Daddy take care of me, you sound as though she were still alive. Do you mean that?" Suzanne held on to Mrs. Parker's arm.

"That's just what I mean." Mrs. Parker said each word slowly and carefully. "Of course, not the way that you are alive for me now, but the way you are alive for me even when you are away at camp and I can't see and touch you.

Alive in love, you might say. Marge is alive in the love that God gives to all His children."

"But, when I'm away at camp," Suzanne protested, "you can at least write me letters."

"I've always believed that prayers to God are something like letters to those we love," Mrs. Parker said quietly.

Suzanne released Mrs. Parker's arm, and folded her hands in her lap. She sat back in silence. Tears rolled slowly down her checks. After a few minutes, Mrs. Parker looked at her watch.

"Oh, my goodness," she said, "the boys will think we're lost. We had better get on home."

Very little was said on the way back. As the car pulled into the Parker driveway, Suzanne turned to her mother.

"Mother, may I take a walk—by myself, I mean? I want to think some more about all we've said. I think it's important, but I'm still a little mixed up."

"Of course you can," Mrs. Parker said, "but be back by supper, please."

Suzanne walked away from her mother with great determination, as though she knew where she was going. When she arrived in front of the church, she looked carefully to be sure that no one saw her. Then she slipped inside and knelt down in the last pew.

CHAPTER SIXTEEN

Tables of Stone

"Before we begin the story of Moses and the burning bush, Jack," Mr. Parker said with a smile, "throw another log on the fire, will you?"

It was a cold, rainy evening in early February. The Parkers were having an indoor picnic. Jack and his father had built a roaring fire in the fireplace while Suzanne and Mrs. Parker set out hot dogs, rolls, and a roasting fork for each member of the family. Although Sammy got the paper cups ready for hot chocolate, mostly he strutted around the house in his "Sammy Parker" jacket which had arrived that morning.

"Sammy, I wish you would take that jacket off," Mrs. Parker pleaded. "You're going to die of the heat when you start to cook your hot dog."

Since it wasn't an order, Sammy ignored his mother's advice. He had waited more than two months for the jacket, and he intended to break it in properly. The jacket stayed on, and buttoned, through two hot dogs and eight marshmallows. When Jack put the new log on the fire, the top two buttons were undone. As Mr. Parker read how God spoke to Moses out of the burning bush, the other four buttons were opened.

He paused to smile at Sammy who, red-faced and perspiring, wiped his forehead with a sleeve of the new jacket. Mr. Parker winked at his wife, and then continued.

Then the LORD said, "I have seen the affliction of my people who are in Egypt, and have heard their cry because of their taskmasters; I know their sufferings, and I have come down to deliver them out of the land of the Egyptians, and to bring them up out of that land to a good and broad land, a land flowing with milk and honey, to the place of the Canaanites. . . ."

"The people of Israel sure needed help," Jack observed, "but it all happened so fast. Gee, last night they were living like millionaires, thanks to Joseph; tonight, they're slaves."

"Of course, an awful lot happened between what we read last night and tonight, Jack," his father replied. "For one thing, a great many years have gone by—the Bible says over four hundred. You know, a great deal can happen in four hundred years . . ."

"Why, four hundred years ago," Mrs. Parker said, "Columbus had just barely discovered America. Look at all that's happened since then."

"After Joseph died," Mr. Parker explained, "a new king came into power in Egypt, who didn't know Joseph, and that's where all the trouble began. Little by little, the Egyptians took away the privileges that Joseph had given his countrymen until, by the time of Moses, the Israelites were no more than slaves. The pharaoh put slavedrivers over the Israelites who, with great cruelty, forced them to build two cities—Pithom and Raamses.

"Well, Moses was an Israelite," Mr. Parker continued, "who was . . ."

"Oh, Daddy," interrupted Suzanne, "we know the story of Moses. Everybody knows the story of Moses."

"Moses was brought up in the pharaoh's house," Jack continued for his father, "and he was treated pretty well, while all the rest of the people of Israel were having a bad time. I guess this must have bothered Moses, because one day he saw an Egyptian whipping an Israelite, and he up and killed him. Then Moses was afraid that he would be punished for what he had done, so he escaped . . ."

". . . into the land of Midian," Mr. Parker finished for him.

"Where's Midian?" Suzanne asked.

"I guess it's time to bring the map out," Mr. Parker said. He pulled the large, thin book out from behind his chair. Setting it on the floor in front of everyone, he opened it to a gaily colored map.

"Now, here's the Land of Goshen," he said, pointing out the part of Egypt in which the Israelites had settled. "Here are the cities of Pithom and Raamses. And way over here is the land of Midian. Moses stayed there with a man named Jethro, and eventually married one of his daughters. Moses tended Jethro's flocks. It was during his stay with Jethro that God spoke to Moses out of the burning bush."

"I'll bet the children could tell us what happens now," Mrs. Parker said.

"Well," Suzanne began, "God tells Moses to go and save the people of Israel by leading them out of Egypt."

"And Moses says, 'Who me?' " Jack pointed his finger at his nose as he spoke.

" 'Yes, you!' " Suzanne continued. " 'Go and speak to the people of Israel in my Name,' God says to Moses."

"But Moses tries to wiggle out of it, doesn't he?" Mr. Parker asked. "He says to God, 'Oh, I couldn't speak to anyone in your Name, because I don't even know what it is.' Then . . .

God said to Moses, "I AM WHO I AM." And he said, "Say this to the people of Israel, 'I AM has sent me to you."

"That's a *name?*" Jack asked.

"It doesn't make any sense to me," Suzanne agreed.

"I think it means, 'I am the One who is not dependent upon anyone,' " Mrs. Parker explained. "By that, I mean . . . well, you three children are here in this family because of Daddy and me, just as Daddy and I are here because of our parents. Each of us is dependent upon people who lived before us. But God is here just because He's God. There was nothing before Him. He's the beginning of everything."

"That's what the first story we read in the Bible said,

didn't it?" Suzanne asked. "You know, that God was there in the beginning before everything else."

"Then it's not a name," Jack interrupted. "It's an explanation."

"It's both, Jack," Mr. Parker said, "just the way all names are both. 'Parker' explains which family you belong to, and 'Jack' explains which one of the Parkers you are. The postman would have a hard time if names weren't explanations also. Isn't that right?"

"I guess so," Jack agreed, "but if you don't mind, I think I'll call Him 'God.' I like it better than 'I AM WHO I AM.' "

"That's O.K. with me, Jack, and I'm sure it's O.K. with Him," Mr. Parker said. "Well now, when Moses' first excuse didn't work, he tried another. He said that the pharaoh and the Israelites still wouldn't believe him, so . . .

The LORD said to him, "What is that in your hand?" He said, "A rod." And he said, "Cast it on the ground." So he cast it on the ground, and it became a serpent; and Moses fled from it. But the LORD said to Moses, "Put out your hand, and take it by the tail"—so he put out his hand and caught it, and it became a rod in his hand . . .

"Hot dog!" Jack shouted, clapping his hands. "The magic begins. But this is *only* the beginning. Wait till he gets to the pharaoh."

"Hold on a minute, Jack," Mr. Parker said. "These really aren't magic tricks. They're signs—proofs of the power of God."

"You mean, these are signs that God is caring for Moses and the children of Israel?" Suzanne asked. "They're more signs of the covenant then, aren't they?"

Mr. Parker nodded his agreement.

"Well, Moses still tries to make excuses," Mr. Parker continued. "Now he says that he can't speak well enough to be a spokesman for God. God tells Moses not to worry, because He will put the right thoughts in his head and the right words in his mouth. Even this doesn't convince Moses, however . . ."

"Oh, my Lord, send, I pray, some other person." Then the anger of the LORD was kindled against Moses and he said, "Is there not Aaron, your brother, the Levite? I know that he can speak well. . . . He shall speak for you to the people; and he shall be a mouth for you . . ."

Mr. Parker paused.

"You know, as I read this the first time, I remembered

Mr. Hall telling me about talking with boys whom he hoped would go into the ministry. He said that he gets all kind of excuses, but the last one is always, 'I can't speak well enough.' Mr. Hall says that the funny part is, when you're on God's business, you can do far more than you think you can."

"Of course, I think that Moses sounds like any one of us when we're asked to do important things," Mrs. Parker said. "We can think up a hundred and one reasons for not trusting God, can't we?"

"I guess Moses finally became convinced," Mr. Parker continued, "because the next thing we know, Moses and Aaron have sold the Israelites on the idea of getting out of Egypt, and they're about to break the news to the pharaoh . . ."

"John," Mrs. Parker interrupted, "I think this is probably a good place to stop. It's getting late."

Mr. Parker closed the Bible with a smack.

"Will Moses meet the pharaoh? Will the stick turn into a snake? Will the pharaoh let the people of Israel go? For the answer to these questions, tune in tomorrow night for the next exciting episode—same time, same station."

Mr. and Mrs. Parker shooed the gang upstairs. They noticed that Sammy was carrying his jacket, and looking much cooler.

The whole next evening was spent on Moses' meetings with the pharaoh. Jack enjoyed every last detail. After the last plague had descended upon the Egyptians, Jack made his father list all nine of them in order: blood, frogs, gnats, flies, cattle disease, boils, hail, locusts, and the death of the first-born.

Mr. Parker reminded his family that, even today, Jewish people have a religious holiday to offer thanks for their deliverance from the last plague. The holiday is called "The Passover," because Jewish children were saved when the plague "passed over" the homes of the people of Israel.

"The holiday actually celebrates the whole deliverance from Egypt," he said, "especially the crossing of the Red Sea. But we won't come to that until tomorrow night."

The following evening began with map-reading. The subject was, "Israel's Escape from Egypt." Mr. Parker pointed out the place from which the Israelites left (near the cities of Pithom and Raamses), and where they were going (the land of Canaan). They were all surprised to discover that the "pillar of cloud" that led the Israelites by day, and the "pillar of fire" that guided them at night, might have been a volcano.

Jack was, of course, delighted when the pharaoh changed his mind again about releasing the Israelites and began to chase them with soldiers and chariots. Even though he knew it was coming, he still thought it was the "greatest" when Moses divided the waters of the Red Sea to let his people through, and then closed them to drown the Egyptians when they tried to follow.

"Friends, I may have some surprising news for you," Mr. Parker said. "Those archaeologists we've talked about say that it probably wasn't the Red Sea the Israelites crossed, but the lake up here called Timsah. The reason they think so is because the words that have been translated as 'Red Sea' actually mean 'Reed Sea' or 'Marsh Sea,' and there weren't any reeds in the Red Sea or in the Gulf of Suez. Also, the Red Sea is too far away to fit into the story. Does this shock anybody?"

"Did the waters still open up to let the Israelites through," Jack asked, "and then close on the Egyptians?"

"There's no reason to think they didn't, Jack," his father replied. "The Bible says that a strong wind drove back the waters . . ."

"Then it doesn't make much difference which water it was, does it?"

Everyone agreed with Jack, so Mr. Parker continued reading. As the wanderings in the wilderness were described, Mrs. Parker commented that if she had been Moses, she would have been fed up with all the complaining. Mr. Parker said it sounded like his family on a long automobile trip, but this suggestion was not accepted.

"I would have told them to go back to Egypt and make bricks without straw," Jack said disgustedly.

"So would I," his father agreed, "but then they never would have escaped from Egypt, would they? I guess it's a good thing God picked Moses and not us."

On the third new moon after the people of Israel had gone forth out of the land of Egypt, on that day they came into the wilderness of Sinai. . . . and there Israel encamped before the mountain. And Moses went up to God, and the LORD called him out of the mountain, saying, "Thus you shall say to the house of Jacob, and tell the people of Israel: You have seen what I did to the Egyptians, and how I bore you on eagles' wings and brought you to myself. Now therefore, if you will obey my voice and keep my covenant, you shall be my own possession among all peoples; for all the earth is mine, and you shall be to me a kingdom of priests and a holy nation. . . ."

"This is beginning to sound more like a two-way deal than anything we've read before," Jack said.

"It seems to me that God's about to ask something

more of Israel than just trusting," Suzanne added. "I guess this is where the Ten Commandments come in."

"That's right, Suzanne," her father agreed. "God does get a bit more definite than He's been before. But, 'trusting' is not easy, you know, and we can all stand some help in it. I think that, here, God is telling Israel what 'trusting' really is. Anyway, let's see . . ."

And the LORD came down upon Mount Sinai, to the top of the mountain; and the LORD called Moses to the top of the mountain, and Moses went up. . . .

And God spoke all these words, saying,

"I am the LORD your God. . . . You shall have no other gods before me.

"You shall not make yourself a graven image. . . .

"You shall not take the name of the LORD your God in vain. . . .

"Remember the sabbath day, to keep it holy. . . .

"Honor your father and your mother. . . .

"You shall not kill.

"You shall not commit adultery.

"You shall not steal.

"You shall not bear false witness against your neighbor.

"You shall not covet. . . ."

The LORD said to Moses, ". . . I will give you tables of stone, with the law and the commandment, which I have written for their instruction."

"Boy, Moses must have needed a quarter-ton truck to get those tables down off the mountain," Jack said.

"I feel sort of funny about it," Suzanne said with a shiver. "It's so *really* definite—and there are so many

'don't's' in it. It's as though this is the final chapter of . . . well, of everything. What I mean is that I feel as though the story of the covenant is finished."

"Oh no, Suzanne," Mr. Parker said, "it's just the opposite. The story of the covenant between God and His people is just beginning with the tables of stone."

"And it's a story," Mrs. Parker said, "that hasn't ended yet."

CHAPTER SEVENTEEN

A New Friend

Magurk was sleepy. Magurk was disgusted!

All this talk, he thought, *all this talk. Who was the first to make friends with him anyway? I was! Let's stop this chatter and go to bed.*

Jack didn't notice how Magurk's head wobbled from sleep, nor did he pay any attention to Magurk's drooping eyelids. He kept right on talking as though Magurk was as interested in the new family across the street as he was. Of course, Magurk *was* interested—but he was sleepy.

Just then, a car turned into the Parker driveway. Jack jumped to the window and peeked out from behind the curtain.

"It's Dad," Jack whispered to Magurk. "He's back from the meeting. Let's open the door just a crack so we can hear what he says to Mother."

Here we go again, Magurk said to himself. *I don't know what all this fuss is about. Nobody got excited when we moved here. What's so special about this new family? And besides,* he thought as he yawned, *I'm getting old and need my sleep . . .*

Magurk sighed and followed Jack to the door. Jack sat cross-legged on the floor and put his ear against the crack so that he wouldn't miss a word that was said downstairs. Magurk put his head in Jack's lap.

"Shhh," Jack told Magurk, "don't make a sound."

Who's going to make a sound? Magurk thought. *Not me! I'm going to sleep.*

And he did.

Downstairs, Mr. Parker slumped into his favorite chair. He loosened his collar and tie and waited for Mrs. Parker to return from the kitchen with a cup of coffee for him.

"Mary," he said as she entered the living room, "adults

can make such fools of themselves. Take tonight, for example. Here was a group of grown men meeting to decide whether someone who bought a house has the right to live in it." He took a sip of coffee and continued, "Such perfect nonsense. I listened to them talk back and forth until I just couldn't stand it any more. So I got up and gave them a piece of my mind . . ."

"Oh, John," interrupted Mrs. Parker, "I hope you didn't say anything you'll regret later."

"I certainly didn't," Mr. Parker said firmly. "What I said was . . ." and he proceeded to describe the whole evening to his wife.

Upstairs, Jack listened intently. Every once in a while he would whisper to Magurk (who was sound asleep), "Boy, that's telling them—eh, Magurk?" As Mr. Parker continued speaking, Jack began to think back to the day when the new family moved in.

About two months ago, the family who lived across the street from the Parkers moved away. Everybody in the neighborhood wondered who was going to buy the house, but they didn't have to wonder for long. Within two weeks, the "For Sale" sign was taken down, and a "Sold" sign put in its place. Two weeks later (on a Saturday morning), a moving truck was parked in front of the house. The new family was moving in.

Jack rushed through breakfast and dashed outside to watch the moving men unload the truck. He and Magurk sat on the curb, being sure to keep out of the way. (Magurk was especially careful, because he remembered all the trouble he had got into when the Parkers moved.) Pretty soon, Jack noticed a boy about his own age come out of the house. He walked to the street and leaned against the side of the truck.

"What's his name?" the new boy said, pointing to Magurk.

"Magurk."

"That's a funny name." The boy squatted down. "Here, boy. Come here, Magurk."

Magurk left Jack's side and trotted over to the new boy. He stopped two or three feet from the boy to be sure everything was all right, and then went right to him. The boy rubbed Magurk's head and patted him on the side.

"Can he do tricks?"

"Some," Jack replied. "What's your name?"

"Tokuji."

" 'Toe-ku-gee'?" Jack repeated. "That's a hard one."

"Most people call me 'Hash,' " the boy said. "That's because my last name's Hashimoto."

" 'Hash'?" Jack said. "Well, that sure is easier than Toe-ku-gee. My name's Jack—Jack Parker."

By the time the rest of Jack's friends arrived on the scene, he and Hash had learned quite a bit about each other. Hash's father was a Nisei Japanese who was an engineer in a large factory. (Hash explained that "Nisei" was pronounced "nee-say" and meant a "Japanese-born-in-America.") Hash collected rocks, too, and he said he'd show Jack his collection as soon as it was unpacked. *And,* he loved to play baseball.

Hash was a very happy person who laughed a great deal. He and Jack liked each other from the very beginning. Jack was anxious to have him meet his friends.

Roger and the other boys liked Hash almost as quickly as Jack did. Even Willy took to him easily, which surprised Jack. But it was Johnny Ridzik who started all the trouble.

"I don't want to play with a Jap," Johnny said.

"He's not a Jap," Jack said. "He's a Japanese-American —a . . . a . . . a Nisei."

"I don't care what name you call it," Johnny said bitterly. "My pop fought in the war against the Japs—and one of them shot him. Maybe it was *his* father who shot my pop."

"My father was in the army, too," Hash said. "He . . ."

"Yeah," interrupted Johnny, "the Japanese Army."

"The American Army," Hash said, getting a little mad. "And he's got two Purple Hearts."

"That's probably a big, fat lie," Johnny shouted at him. "We don't want you around here. Why don't you go back where you came from?"

"I came from Denver, Colorado," Hash said.

"Well, go back where your father came from."

"He came from Los Angeles, California."

"Well," Johnny said, "your grandfather, then."

"Where did your grandfather come from?" Hash asked him.

Roger spoke up. "His grandfather came from Poland. He told us that."

"Well, then," Hash said, "let's both go back to where our grandfathers came from. O.K.?"

"Why, you dirty . . ." Johnny lunged forward and swung at Hash.

It all happened so fast that the other boys could hardly believe their eyes. All of a sudden Johnny was lying flat on his back about four feet away from Hash. He got up and charged again. Hash didn't seem to do anything—but there was Johnny, flat on his back a second time. He got up to charge again, and then thought better of it. Hash walked over to him.

"Let's shake hands and be friends. What do you say?"

"I say 'Nuts,' " Johnny replied and walked away from them all.

"Hey, Hash," Roger said, clapping him on the back, "that was great. What did you do to him?"

"That was *Judo*," said an adult voice behind them.

"Hi, Dad," Hash said. "These are my new friends." And he introduced his father to Jack, Roger, Willy, and the other Raiders.

"What's *Judo,* Mr. Ha . . . Hashi . . . Mr. Hash?" laughed Jack.

"Well, it's an art of self-defense. It's part of a way-of-life the Japanese call *Bushido*."

" 'Boo-she-doe'?" questioned Roger.

"Early Japan had knights, you know," Mr. Hashimoto explained, "and they were very much like King Arthur's Knights of the Round Table. They agreed on some rules for living that they called *Bushido*—which means 'the way of a knight.' *Judo* was a part of this. But it was to be used only in self-defense. If any Japanese knight used *Judo* to start a fight, he would be punished."

"The way I would have been punished," Hash said, "if Johnny hadn't swung at me first."

"Boy-oh-boy!" Roger said. "I think it would be neat to know *Judo*—for self-defense, of course."

"My father could teach you," Hash said. "He taught me."

"I'll bet we all would like to learn," Jack said enthusiastically. "Wouldn't we, fellows?"

Everybody agreed.

"I suppose I could give you lessons in *Judo*—sometime," Mr. Hashimoto said hesitantly.

"When?" they all shouted.

Mr. Hashimoto laughed, and it was finally agreed that next Saturday morning he would give them all the first lesson—on the condition that it would only be used for self-defense. The boys gave their solemn promise to this, and then went off for their Saturday morning game of baseball.

At supper that night, Jack told his father and mother all about the day's happenings. Mrs. Parker was afraid the boys would get hurt learning *Judo,* but Mr. Parker thought that the *Judo* lessons sounded like a good idea.

"Nonsense, Mary," Mr. Parker said. "I learned *Judo* during the war. It will teach the boys how to take care of themselves."

Two nights later, it was a very worried Jack who sat down at the supper table.

"Dad," he said to Mr. Parker, "can you force a person to move out of a neighborhood?"

"Not that I know of, Son. Why?"

"Well, Johnny Ridzik told us in school today that his father was going to get everybody in the neighborhood to sign a piece of paper that would make Hash and his family move away from here. He said he didn't want to live with foreigners."

"I haven't heard about this," Mr. Parker said seriously, "but I'll let you know if I do."

Mr. Parker heard the next day. A meeting was being held that night to which all the men in the neighborhood were invited. Mr. Ridzik wouldn't say why he was calling the meeting, only that there was a very serious problem to consider.

"John," Mrs. Parker said, "you're not going to get mixed up in that, are you?"

"You bet your life I am," Mr. Parker replied angrily. "I'm not going to let anyone tell me whom I can have for neighbors."

"Dad," Jack said anxiously, "you won't let them send the Hash family away, will you? We like them. Hash is a real good guy."

"They're not going to do anything to them," Mr. Parker said to Jack. "Not if I can help it, they're not."

After supper, Mr. Parker left for the meeting. Jack was so worried he couldn't concentrate on his homework.

When time came to turn out the lights, he couldn't go to sleep. He decided to wait up for his father to return. And he decided that Magurk would keep him company.

* * *

The sound of his father's voice snapped Jack out of his daydreaming. Magurk's head was still in his lap. Jack's ear was still tight against the crack in the door, and he listened closely as his father told Mrs. Parker about the meeting.

". . . so I said to them," Mr. Parker concluded, "that as a citizen of a free country, all I asked of a man was that he be a good neighbor. And that as a man who believed in God (Mary, just think of me sounding like a preacher), I have no right to judge a child of His because he looks a little different from me. The Hashimoto's are members of God's family as fully as we are. So I told them that I would have no part of this, and I started to leave.

"You know, Mary," Mr. Parker said, "they applauded me and all but three of them left with me. No one's going to do anything to our new neighbors."

The sound of applause came down from upstairs. Jack was so proud that he just sat by the door clapping his hands. The noise woke up Magurk. Both Mr. and Mrs. Parker stopped talking.

"Who's making that noise?" called Mr. Parker.

Jack crept sheepishly downstairs, with Magurk sleepily following him.

"Gee, Dad," he said, "you were great."

CHAPTER EIGHTEEN

Lent and Easter

" 'Do something constructive,' 'do something constructive,' " Suzanne said disgustedly. "Oh, that's what ministers tell you every year at this time."

"Yeah," chimed in Jack, "but they never tell you any *interesting* things to do—just stuff like saying prayers or reading the Bible. Heck, we do that already."

"M-o-t-h-e-r," Suzanne whined, "what *can* we do?"

The next day was Ash Wednesday, and Jack and Suzanne were talking with their mother about what they should "give up" for Lent. Suzanne said she was giving up chocolates and desserts, because she was getting too fat. Jack said he just couldn't decide.

Mrs. Parker told Suzanne that if she was getting too fat (which she wasn't), then she ought to give up sweets—but not to blame it on Lent. And, she went on to say, if Jack wasn't sure of what to do, then maybe this was something they both ought to think about seriously. Jack and Suzanne agreed.

"It ought to be something hard," Jack said.

". . . and something special," continued Suzanne.

". . . and something constructive," added Mrs. Parker.

They all sat in silence and thought. It was a long time before anyone spoke. Finally, Mrs. Parker made a suggestion.

"How about trying to love someone we don't love?"

"That's a swell idea," Jack said enthusiastically. "We could try to love Sammy."

"Oh Jack," laughed Mrs. Parker, "that wouldn't be hard—because you really love Sammy. Sometimes you may get a bit peeved at him . . ." Mrs. Parker paused, and then said, "I mean someone who is *really* hard to love."

They all sat and thought some more, chins in hands.

"Let me ask you both a question," Mrs. Parker said. "Think of all your schoolmates. Is there one of them who's especially *hard* to love?"

Jack and Suzanne both shouted, "Willy," at the same time.

"Well now," Mrs. Parker said slowly, "there's a thought."

"Oh, now look, Mom," Jack said. "We wanted something hard—not something *impossible.*"

"Jack's right, Mother," Suzanne said. "It's hard enough just to *stand* Willy, but to *love* him . . ."

"You've both just given me two very good reasons why you should spend this Lent trying to love . . ." Mrs. Parker thought for a minute. "No, not 'trying to love,' but really *loving* Willy. If it's hard to do," she added, "that makes it an even better thing to do for Lent."

"But Mother," Suzanne protested, "you just don't KNOW him!"

"I know that God loves all of His children, and that He wants us to follow His example in love. There are times when we all are hard to love—even you, my dears —but these times are something like thermometers: they tell us just how much we need to be loved. If Willy is hard to love a lot of the time, I think that's probably a pretty good sign that he really *needs* to be loved.

"Anyway," Mrs. Parker said, "I'll bet you could do it just for Lent—couldn't you?"

Jack and Suzanne agreed reluctantly and, together with Mrs. Parker, they plotted their strategy.

The next few weeks were full of ups and downs, successes and failures. For Suzanne, at times it meant saying nothing when she wanted to shout nasty replies to Willy's teasing. (She found that if she counted to ten before saying anything, it helped.) At other times, she had to search very hard for nice things to say to Willy when the other kids were saying mean things to him.

"It's very strange, Mother," Suzanne said one day when Lent was almost over, "but it's not as hard to be nice to him now as it was at the beginning."

It was Jack, though, who had the hardest time. He had to do all the things Suzanne did—only more. This was because Suzanne was a girl and didn't have to play with Willy all the time. But Willy was a member of the Red Raiders, and Jack had to work at loving him all day long. Or, at least it seemed that way.

"You know, Dad," Jack said to his father one night, "I always thought Willy wanted to be *the* most important person there was. I mean, I thought that he always wanted to be chosen first—before anybody else. (That's why we always chose him last.)"

"And doesn't he?" Mr. Parker asked.

"Well, as I said, we always used to choose him last, but today I chose him third. I didn't choose him first, because he's not the best player, and I didn't choose him last, because he's not the worst. I chose him third, because that's just about how good he is."

"That sounds reasonable," Jack's father said.

"And, you know, it's funny," Jack continued, "he wasn't mean or fresh or anything all afternoon. In fact, he played better than he has for a long time. It beats me!"

Almost every day, Jack and Suzanne would talk with Mrs. Parker about how the day went with Willy and, at night, they always remembered him in their family prayers. By the week before Easter, they all agreed that maybe Willy wasn't as hard to love as they had thought.

"And, you know what, Mother?" Jack asked. "It seems as though the other kids are being nicer to him too."

"That's right," Suzanne agreed.

"I've always heard that love is like a cold—it's catching," laughed Mrs. Parker. "Maybe it is."

On Palm Sunday, it seemed as though the "love-Willy" Lenten discipline had been successfully completed. Jack and Suzanne came home from church just bubbling over with enthusiasm. Never had Willy been so pleasant and never had the other children been so nice to him. Even the teacher agreed that it was the best church school class they had ever had.

"It worked, Mother," Suzanne said happily.

". . . and Lent isn't even finished," Jack added. "We're ahead of schedule."

That was Sunday. Monday was different.

The acolytes were meeting to practice for the Easter services. Jack was late, and, as he climbed the stairs to the sacristy, he heard the boys teasing Willy.

"What's the matter, Willy," one of them said, "you been sick or something?"

"Yeah," said another, "you've been so nice we didn't hardly know you."

Willy had listened to all this in silence and was about to reply, when Jack stepped into the room.

"Leave him alone," Jack said.

"Who do you think you are—his mother?" Jimmy Bivins said.

"I'm the guy who's going to poke you in the nose if you don't lay off Willy," Jack said belligerently.

"Just try it," challenged Jimmy.

So Jack did. Jimmy left the room with his nose bleeding. When Mr. Hall came in a few minutes later, he took the roll and wanted to know where Jimmy was.

"Jimmy had to go home," Roger said. Nobody else said anything.

When Jack told his mother about the fight, he said, "I

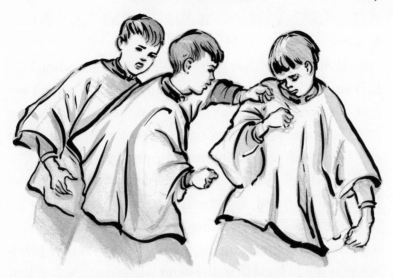

really didn't want to hit him, but I just got mad. If it had happened on the baseball field, maybe I wouldn't have done anything. But there we were in church . . ."

"Well, Jack," Mrs. Parker said, "I don't know whether it was right or not. We'll have to think about it a bit."

"Mom," Jack said hesitantly, "could we . . . could we have Willy over for supper some night?"

Willy came to supper that Thursday. At the table, he sat between Jack and Suzanne. He was about to start eating when Mr. Parker said,

"It's our family custom to hold hands for grace, Willy."

They all held hands and bowed their heads.

"The eyes of all wait upon thee, O Lord," began Mr.

Parker and, except for Willy, everybody said the responses.

"I didn't know that grace," Willy said, sounding embarrassed. "In fact, I don't know any grace. We don't say it at our house."

"That's one of our favorites," Mrs. Parker said. "You can find it (if you want) near the end of Psalm 145."

"I liked it," Willy said, "and I liked the prayer Mr. Parker said after it. Especially," he said, staring into his lap, "the part about thanking God for good friends."

It was a most pleasant evening. In fact, it was so pleasant that it was hard to understand what happened on Friday. Like most arguments, Jack later found it difficult to remember what they were arguing about. All he knew was that he and Willy were playing, then they were arguing, and Jack found himself saying to Willy,

"That's all the thanks a guy gets. I've spent all Lent trying to be nice to you . . ."

He got no further. Willy's face turned pale and he stood as though he were made of stone.

"Drop dead," he shouted at Jack. "I don't need anybody to be *nice* to me."

He turned and ran away from Jack.

Jack was furious as he told his mother about what happened. She listened quietly while he raved on, and then she said,

"Sometimes when we're 'nice' to a person, we're really being 'sorry' for them. Maybe Willy didn't want anybody to be sorry for him. It's hard to learn, but there's a difference between being 'nice' to someone and 'loving' them."

Jack walked away from his mother without saying anything. He didn't go out to play with the boys the next day, but stayed in his room trying to work on his rock collection. He didn't see Willy again until Sunday morning.

The Parker family had just arrived at church when Willy crossed the street. He was alone. At first, Jack looked the other way and started up the church steps. Then he stopped and went back down to meet Willy.

"I'm sorry," Jack said to him. "Let's be friends—really."

"I'd like that," replied Willy with a big smile.

They shook hands and went into the church together.